"Were you looking for me, Jamie?"

Cade stood in the hallway wearing only a pair of briefs, dark hair slightly tousled from sleep, sleek shoulders looming powerfully in the shadows. "What woke you?" he asked softly.

The words soothed and beckoned, promising warmth and passion in place of irrational fear. "I—I had a bad dream," she whispered, hugging her arms to her breasts.

"Did you? Come here, sweetheart, and I'll help you forget all about it." He held out a strong square hand.

Jamie trembled, but not from fear. Heart racing, she slowly put out her own hand.

"You won't have any nightmares in my bed," he promised huskily, tugging her gently forward. "I'll make certain all your dreams are deeply satisfying...."

"Jayne Ann Krentz entertains to the hilt..."
                                        —Catherine Coulter

JAYNE ANN KRENTZ

TRUE COLORS

MIRA

ISBN 1-55166-798-3

TRUE COLORS

Copyright © 1986 by Jayne Ann Krentz.

MIRA and the Star Colophon are trademarks used under license and registered
in Australia, New Zealand, Philippines, United States Patent and Trademark
Office and in other countries.

Visit us at www.mirabooks.com

Printed in U.S.A.

For Birgit Davis-Todd,
who edits with precision, conciseness
and a sense of polish. My thanks.

ONE

The reporters descended like a swarm of vampire bats, surrounding the tomato-red Audi before Jamie Garland could even get the door open. A flash of the simmering anger she had been trying to control for three days slammed through her. With all her strength she shoved at the Audi door. When that didn't work she leaned back and braced one foot against it.

"Come on, Miss Isabel, we'll have to make a run for it." The door gave slowly as the press of photographers, newsmen and related vultures jockeyed for position.

"My God," the older woman sitting beside Jamie breathed in genuine shock, "where did all these people come from?"

"These aren't exactly people, Miss Isabel," Jamie informed her caustically. "They're reporters." She got the door open a little farther, and a microphone was shoved in her face. Jamie ignored it, reaching behind her for Miss Isabel's hand. "Get out on my side of the car and stay close. Don't say anything, just concentrate on making a dash for the front door, understand?"

Isabel Fitzgerald's old-fashioned silver bun bobbed as she nodded. "I understand. But why are they here?" Her bewildered gray eyes swept the loud crowd.

"They want a story," Jamie said bluntly.

"About Hadley?"

"I'm afraid so."

"But how could they know so soon?" Isabel whispered sadly as she inched across the seat in Jamie's wake.

"The same way the authorities knew to walk in and seize Hadley's records and books yesterday," Jamie told her grimly. "Cade Santerre must have let them in on the results of his brilliant investigative work."

Isabel gasped. "Surely Mr. Santerre wouldn't have informed the press and sent them down on us like this? He always seemed like such a nice man, even if he did..." She couldn't finish the sentence.

Jamie drew a deep breath as she shoved once more against the car door with her sandaled foot. "Mr. Santerre is the kind of man who does anything he wants, regardless of who gets hurt. He's a ruthless—" she paused to slide out of the opening she had created, dragging Isabel behind her "—conniving, lying, deceitful son of a..."

"Would you repeat that into the mike, Miss Garland?" a reporter demanded. "And tell us whom you were describing, please."

Before Jamie could tell the man that she could easily

have been describing one of the fraternity of newspeople who surrounded the car, a dark growl of a voice intervened.

"Leave her alone," Cade Santerre ordered, pushing three photographers aside as he waded through the crush toward Jamie and Miss Isabel. "She doesn't want to talk to the press."

"Our readers deserve answers. Some of them were among Hadley Fitzgerald's victims," a woman reporter snapped. She edged toward Isabel, reportage instincts telling her the older woman was the weaker prey. "Miss Fitzgerald, we understand you're a painter. How involved were you in your brother's tax-shelter schemes?"

"I had no idea," Miss Isabel whispered despairingly. "I mean, I never knew anything about it. I'm sure there's an explanation for it all. Hadley would never do such a thing."

"What about you, Miss Garland?" Another microphone blocked Jamie's path. "Is it true you were Fitzgerald's private secretary? His mistress? True that he confided everything in you and that you helped him in the fraud?"

"I said leave her alone," Santerre gritted, reaching Jamie's side at last. His fingers closed around her arm.

Jamie flinched as the strong, blunt hand chained her to Cade's side. Memories of the last time he had touched her flamed in her mind. That had been two nights ago. Then the strength in his hands had been a source of wonder and excitement. He had wielded his masculine power so easily, Jamie recalled with a vivid clarity that stained her cheeks even now. So very easily. And she had been such a fool, giving him everything she had to give; both promises and passion. Neither, it seemed, meant much to Cade Santerre.

With his free hand Cade grasped the quivering Isabel and started on a path toward the front door of the beautiful Fitzgerald home. In spite of themselves, reporters and photographers gave way before the implacable, savage intent reflected clearly in Santerre's unyielding features.

"Don't do us any favors, Cade," Jamie hissed as she was hauled through the jostling crowd. "It's a little late for that kind of thing."

"These guys are like vultures," Cade muttered, guiding the two women up the flagstone walk.

"I can deal with vultures," Jamie retorted, ignoring one particularly persistent cameraman who was running alongside. "After all, they don't show up until after the kill. It's the predator who brings down the victim in the first place who's really dangerous."

"I assume it was me you were describing a minute ago when you climbed out of the car?" Cade observed as they reached the front door. He waited with obvious impatience while Jamie sorted out the right key. Miss Isabel clung to his arm, peering around anxiously. When one or two newsmen tried to move in again Cade warded them off with a chilling glance. Santerre had the kind of eyes well suited to such glances, Jamie thought vaguely. They were a feral, tawny brown, laced with small flecks of gold. The eyes of a hunting cat.

"I'm...I'm quite sure Jamie didn't mean you, Mr. Santerre," Miss Isabel hastened to assure him as she ducked her head to avoid a camera. Even in a crisis her good manners and fundamental faith in people came to the fore.

"Of course I meant him," Jamie said coldly as she turned the key in the lock. "Who else do we know who fits the description so perfectly?"

"Jamie, I've got to talk to you." Cade reached over her shoulder to push open the door. He urged both women through into the hall and then slammed the door shut again, right in the face of the aggressive cameraman.

Jamie ignored Cade, her attention on her employer. She spoke gently to the older woman. "Go on upstairs, Miss Isabel. You need to rest. You didn't sleep last night and you've had a horrible day. I'll be up in a little while with some hot tea."

Miss Isabel looked uneasily at her personal assistant and then at the grim-faced man standing behind her. "Are you quite sure, dear? I don't mind staying down here if you'd rather not talk to Mr. Santerre alone."

"She's perfectly safe with me," Cade muttered.

Jamie nodded in agreement, her eyes narrowed behind the lenses of her stylish oversize glasses. "That's right, Miss Isabel. I'm quite safe with Cade now. He's already gotten everything he wanted from me. Go on upstairs. You need some rest."

She sensed behind her Cade's sharply indrawn breath, but he said nothing as Miss Isabel walked slowly up the carpeted stairs and disappeared. Jamie watched her sadly. She'd never seen her employer in such a condition. The older woman appeared astonishingly frail today. Her normal energy and enthusiasm had been drowned beneath the weight of shock and worry. And there was nothing Jamie could do except try to offer support and friendship. Her own sense of guilt just made the situation all the more depressing.

Jamie waited as long as possible, but when she heard the door to her employer's room close she knew she could no longer delay facing Cade Santerre. Summoning up the full extent of what remained of her inner fortitude, she swung around and confronted the man who had made passionate love to her only two nights ago.

"Why are you still hanging around, Cade? Haven't you done enough damage?"

"I'm not leaving until I've made you understand exactly what happened," he vowed harshly. "It wasn't supposed to end like this. I've been trying to tell you that since yesterday but you wouldn't even take my calls. That's why I'm here. I'm going to talk to you, Jamie, and you, by God, are going to listen!" He shoved his blunt fingers through the gray-flecked brown pelt of his hair and stalked across the sleekly beautiful, elegantly modern living room.

Hadley Fitzgerald's Santa Barbara home had appeared an ideal place to spend the summer, or so Jamie had thought two months ago when she had arrived with Miss Isabel. The Pacific Ocean was almost at their front door, and the warmth of a California beach summer had seemed to hold so much promise. In the summer Santa Barbara was alive with artists, craftspeople and tourists. The charm of the town's Spanish architecture combined with the picturesque locale to create a California fantasy. Jamie realized she had taken Cade Santerre's hand and stepped all too willingly into that inviting fantasy. But now the chill of fall was in the air, hastened by the same man who had created the warmth. Jamie eyed him uneasily as Santerre came to a halt by the wall of windows that looked out on a serene Japanese-inspired garden.

Cade Santerre had transformed a pleasant working vacation at the beach into a passionate summer affair that had culminated in a night of shimmering love. That had been two evenings ago. The next day, yesterday, he had destroyed Jamie's newfound world of light and magic, leaving it in a pile of glittering shards at her feet. Only the need to protect her employer had kept Jamie functioning during the past forty-eight hours. She had focused everything on her job. Never had Isabel needed her more.

Jamie studied the man by the window, trying to see him with new, more realistic eyes. But there was little about him that she didn't already know far too intimately. It was just that she had either ignored the evidence that had been before her for the past two months or else she had chosen to interpret it falsely. Fantasies were tricky that way. And heaven knew she'd always tended to view reality from a gentle perspective.

Cade's tawny gold eyes still mirrored cool intelligence and unwavering intent. It was her own fault, Jamie told herself, that she hadn't labeled that gaze with the proper adjective. Ruthless was the word that truly described those eyes.

He was not a particularly good-looking man, but the stamp of inner strength and power was plain on his bluntly hewn features. That same strength and power was echoed in the compact, smoothly muscled body. Jamie closed her eyes briefly, remembering the feel of that body as Cade had crushed her passionately into the tangled sheets. Fleeting pictures of how the moon had gleamed through the yacht's cabin window behind his sleek shoulders came back along with the memory of the rhythmic motion of the sea. Her own husky promise returned to taunt her. *I'll come with you, Cade. If you really want me, I'll come with you.* But he hadn't really wanted her to sail away with him. Cade had been merely making the seduction total. He had wanted complete surrender and he had gotten it from her. Cade was a very thorough man, she had learned.

Frantically she pushed aside the disturbing images, trying to concentrate on the man he really was, not the fantasy lover he had been two nights previously. Today he was dressed in jeans and a dark olive long-sleeved pullover that emphasized the hard lines of stomach and thigh. He always seemed to be casually dressed, Jamie realized, but, then, that was true of just about everyone here in Santa Barbara during the summer. Cade's clothing hadn't gotten in the way of convincing Hadley Fitzgerald that he had money, a great deal of it. Of course, the crisp clean lines of the expensive yacht tethered in the nearby marina had lent credence to the image.

"You fooled us all, didn't you, Cade?" Jamie observed softly. "Hadley, me, even Miss Isabel. You probably missed your calling. You should have gone on the stage. But perhaps that line of work doesn't pay as well as the betrayal business."

He spun around, his movement quick and highly controlled. The tawny gold eyes glittered for an instant. "I didn't betray you, Jamie. I don't care what else you choose to believe about me, I didn't mean for you to get caught in this mess. I want you to know that. Know it and believe it."

She nodded thoughtfully, straining inwardly to keep the leash on her fury and despair. Whatever it cost her, she would not lose her self-control in front of this man. Not again. That night of abandon in his arms had been quite enough. Slowly she walked across the room and sank down onto the white leather banquette that fronted the fireplace.

"Whatever you say, Cade. Would you mind leaving now? I've got a job to do. I'm still working for Miss Isabel, remember?"

The tension in him radiated across the room but he didn't move. "Don't you dare sit there and pretend that it's all over. You know better than that, Jamie."

"Do I?" She met his eyes unflinchingly. "Let's see, this is the day I was going to sail away into the sunset with you, wasn't it? It's difficult to keep the schedule straight. So much has happened recently. But I believe the scenario went something like this: I was going to explain to Miss Isabel that I had to take some time off without any notice because you were being called away on business and you wanted me to come with you. You couldn't leave without me, I think that was how you expressed it. You were quite certain Miss Isabel wouldn't mind me taking a little impromptu vacation. After all, she approved of you. She thought our little romance was charming. You didn't know how long you were going to be gone and you couldn't take the risk of leaving me behind here in Santa Barbara. I assumed, naturally, that you were so passionately captivated by me that you couldn't bear to be without me, not even for a few weeks. You spin a lovely fantasy, Cade. I believed you in the end. I believed you completely. It's incredible now when I think about it, but I was actually prepared to give up everything for you. If you'd asked me to quit my job entirely I probably would have done it."

"Everything I promised was the truth," Cade bit out savagely. "I was going to take you with me. I had it all planned, Jamie. If the people I was working with hadn't screwed up the whole operation at the last minute, you would have been safely out of the picture when the authorities and the reporters moved in on Fitzgerald. I meant to keep you out of it completely. I wanted to protect you."

She widened her eyes behind her glasses, the bitter mockery plain in the gray-green depths of her gaze. "Why would you want to keep me out of it when I had been so much a part of everything up to this point? After all, I'm the one who so stupidly and unintentionally kept you informed of Hadley's comings and goings, wasn't I? I'm the one who was dumb enough to mention his second office here at the house. I'm the one whom you so casually pumped for so much useful information. Surely I deserve to be here at the end. I'm only surprised you didn't have me arrested when Hadley himself slipped through your fingers."

"Don't be a fool. You know damn well I never meant to implicate you."

"Don't tell me you're so naive that you thought you could drag Hadley Fitzgerald down into the mud and not get Miss Isabel and me splattered, too! Do you know what they're saying about me in the papers this morning? They're speculating on whether or not I was Hadley's mistress. That's a joke, isn't it? No one seems to have figured out that I was your mistress, not Hadley's. They're also speculating about Miss Isabel, wondering how much she knew about what was going on. The fact that she's a rather successful painter makes her fair game as far as the press is concerned. She's got a name they can work with, after all. I'm just a nobody who will probably be forgotten fairly quickly. But Miss Isabel's career could suffer because of this."

"Her career won't suffer. Artists can always use a little notoriety. And before I leave here today I'll make damn certain those reporters know you weren't Fitzgerald's mistress!"

"I'd appreciate it if you didn't accomplish that by telling them the truth! I have even less desire to be known as your mistress than as Hadley's. My God, but you're callous," Jamie whispered starkly. "How could

I have ever believed you cared for me? I'll bet you've never cared for another living soul in your whole life!"

"Jamie, you're upset and I can understand that," Cade began carefully, clearly trying to hold on to his temper. "You've been through a lot in the past couple of days."

"No kidding? I must say one hasn't lived until one innocently opens the door bright and early in the morning and finds a man outside holding a search warrant. It does add a certain level of excitement to the scene when a team of government financial investigators walks in right behind him and proceeds to confiscate just about everything of a personal and private nature they can get their hands on!"

"They were only after Fitzgerald's records. After all, they're out to prove fraud, remember? Don't exaggerate, Jamie. They didn't take anything personal and private of yours, did they? Or of Miss Isabel's."

She threw him a derisive look. "Sorry if I seem to be embroidering the issue a bit. Wouldn't want to bore you. It's just that I get so little excitement in my life. When something like this comes along I want to get all the charge out of it that I can. It's not every day that a man seduces me for information he can use to set a trap for someone I happen to like."

"I didn't use you!" Cade exploded roughly.

"No? That's sure what it felt like."

"Those agents weren't supposed to show up on the Fitzgerald doorstep until tomorrow. The whole operation got fouled up when some fool higher up made an executive decision to carry it out two days early.

That's what you've got to understand, Jamie. I had everything planned so that you'd be clear when the roof fell in on Fitzgerald."

"I don't believe you, but even if I did, do you honestly think that would make me feel one bit better about being used?" she demanded furiously. "And what about Miss Isabel? Did you have any plans to protect her?"

Cade stared at Jamie intently, utter ruthlessness underlining every hard feature in his face. "You were the only one I was worried about protecting. I'm a realist. There was no way to save Miss Isabel from being hurt. She's Fitzgerald's sister, his only living relative, so she was bound to get caught up in the scandal. The best thing she could do for herself now is take a long cruise somewhere. You should probably get her out of the country until the whole thing blows over."

"Your suggestion comes a bit late, but we'll certainly consider it," Jamie shot back, privately thinking that it really was a good idea. Perhaps she would mention it to Miss Isabel later.

Cade took a step toward her but halted when she went very still on the white banquette. "Jamie, I did what I had to do. I tried to set things up so that you wouldn't be here when the authorities moved in, but something went wrong. I'm sorry about that part of it. I swear it. I didn't plan for things to go that way."

She lifted her chin challengingly. "My only consolation is knowing that Hadley got away. You really blew it there at the last, didn't you? You were so busy seducing me the other night that you forgot to double

check to see if Mr. Fitzgerald had made any last minute changes in his plans. I could have told you that he
left unexpectedly for San Diego a few days early."

"I didn't seduce you in order to gain information."
Cade ignored Jamie's sharp exclamation of disbelief.
"The original plans would have worked out just fine if
everyone had followed orders. Fitzgerald was supposed to be back tomorrow," Cade said heavily. "And
the authorities weren't supposed to close in until after
we were sure he was back. That idiot Gallagher has a
lot to answer for. We had Fitzgerald in the bag. If Gallagher hadn't decided to play Lone Ranger, we'd have
had Fitzgerald as well as the documents."

"Gallagher being the one who made the decision to
act yesterday? Well, as far as I'm concerned, more
power to Gallagher!"

Cade's expression was hawklike. "While you're
cheering for Hadley Fitzgerald's side, you might spare
a couple of thoughts for all the people he bilked. Miss
Isabel's charming, gentlemanly brother cleared hun-
dreds of thousands of dollars on his tax-shelter
schemes. None of the victims is likely to get his money
back, either, especially now that Fitzgerald himself has
escaped. He's probably out of the country by now."

Jamie drew in a steadying breath. Her palms felt
damp from nerves and tension. "I only have your
word that Hadley was guilty of fraud and, quite
frankly, Cade, your word isn't worth much around
here these days. You've been lying to me and to the
Fitzgeralds for almost two months. What's more, you
put me in an untenable position. How do you think I

feel knowing that I was unwittingly supplying you with information about Miss Isabel's brother? I work for the woman, Cade, and you made me betray the person she cares most about in the world. You used me and I swear I'll never forgive you for that. But I doubt that matters to you, does it? Why should you care what I think about you now? You've got everything you wanted, with the exception of Hadley, of course! But I'm sure you're enough of a *realist* to know that we seldom get absolutely everything we want in life."

Cade moved abruptly, striding across the white Italian tile floor to where Jamie sat on the banquette. She tried to shrink back out of reach but she didn't move quickly enough. Familiar strong fingers locked around her wrist, drawing her to her feet. Cade held her firmly in front of him, his hands gripping her shoulders. Jamie could feel the tightly controlled anger and frustrated tension in him.

"Let's get one thing clear, Jamie Garland. I'm going to say this once more and that's all. You were not responsible for betraying your employer's brother. Hadley Fitzgerald sealed his own fate the day he tried to pull his scam on my sister and her husband."

"Your sister!"

"She and her husband poured twenty thousand dollars into one of Fitzgerald's mining ventures. Unlike some of his clients, Meg and Bill couldn't afford to take that kind of loss. Especially not with a new baby to plan for. When they realized what they'd done they asked me to see if there was any way to get the money back. I started checking into Fitzgerald's operations and realized he wasn't just a fast-talking salesman; he was a crook."

"You were qualified to make that kind of judgment?" Jamie blazed passionately.

"Yes."

She blinked owlishly at the single word, not knowing how to argue the point further. She was only beginning to realize just how little she actually knew about Cade Santerre. It was frightening to acknowledge that after two months of seeing him and after that night in his bed she really knew nothing about him. What a fool she had been. "It sounds to me as though you decided to institute some kind of personal vendetta against Hadley just because your relatives were unwise enough to invest money they couldn't afford in a high-risk venture."

"They weren't involved in a legitimate high-risk deal," Cade rasped impatiently. "They got conned. There's a difference. I decided to go after Hadley and at least put him out of business, even if I couldn't get Meg and Bill's money back for them."

"And I was a convenient tool, wasn't I? Don't try to deny it. You came to Santa Barbara posing as a wealthy vacationing executive investigating ways of shielding his taxable income and Hadley took you on as a client. But you didn't stop there. You started dating me. You admired Miss Isabel's paintings. You took Hadley for cruises in your boat. You made yourself a friend of the Fitzgeralds and a—" She broke off, unable to put the rest into words.

Cade had no such inhibitions. "And a lover to you," he concluded evenly. "Jamie, you must believe me. I didn't plan that part of the operation. It happened. But our relationship had nothing to do with closing the trap on Fitzgerald."

"I don't believe you. I can't believe you. Are you going to deny that you pumped me for information whenever we went out together?"

Cade's eyes narrowed. "I did what had to be done. I'm a practical man and I wanted to bring down Fitzgerald as quickly as possible. No, I'm not going to deny that I asked you a few casual questions and got some useful answers, but the end result would have been the same. I was out to close down Fitzgerald's operations and I would have done it regardless of whether or not you answered a few questions."

Jamie felt as if she would break into a thousand pieces. Pain and fury seemed to be fighting for control within her. "You're a practical man, a realist. You do what has to be done." Cade stood motionless as she flung his incriminating words back at him in a scathing tone. "You use whatever tools come to hand and I certainly came to hand, didn't I? I was right in your palm. But was it really necessary to take the seduction of Jamie Garland all the way? Couldn't you have called a halt before humiliating me completely?"

"What the hell do you mean, humiliating you?" he grated.

"You let me make a complete fool of myself the other night on your damn boat!"

"I made love to you. I didn't make a fool out of you!"

"Somehow it seems to have amounted to the same thing!" she shot back violently. "Why, Cade? Why did you do it? You knew what was going to happen. Except for the fact that your pal Gallagher seems to have fouled up his end, your plans were in place and ready to be carried out. You didn't have to make your victory so complete. But you did it anyway because you're a thorough man, aren't you? A ruthless, arrogant, deceitful but thorough man!"

"I made love to you the other night because I wanted you," he said between clenched teeth. "And because I needed to make certain you would come with me on the boat today for your own protection. I thought that once we'd been together in bed you would—" He snapped off the end of the sentence, aware that what he was about to say would only infuriate Jamie more.

But Jamie wasn't about to let the words remain unsaid. She knew exactly how to finish the sentence. "You thought that after you'd taken me to bed I'd be even more in your power, didn't you? You thought that by seducing me completely you could control me completely. What I don't understand is why you were worried about having that kind of control unless..." Shock went through her. "Unless," she continued very slowly, "you were afraid that something might go wrong at the last minute with your precious operation and you wanted to cover all the bases. That was it, wasn't it? If Hadley did manage to escape you wanted to make sure you still had a spy planted in the household. And that's why you're here now, isn't it? Hadley did slip away and you're looking for a way to find him if and when he tries to contact Miss Isabel."

Grim lines marked the edges of Cade's mouth as he stared down at her. "You're letting your emotions and your anger run away with you, Jamie. I didn't plan anything of the sort."

"Get out of here, Cade. You're not going to get any more from me or from the Fitzgeralds," Jamie said, her eyes unnaturally bright behind her glasses. "I won't play the fool for you again. You obviously have a very low opinion of my intelligence if you think I will. But, then, I guess I haven't given you much reason to think highly of my intellectual abilities, have I?"

"Jamie, you won't even let yourself try to understand. You're allowing your pride and your temper to control your thinking." Cade pulled her stiff, resisting body against his chest, aware that his own frayed temper was almost at the breaking point. For the past two days nothing had gone right. Gallagher had botched the job. Jamie felt used and betrayed. And he, Cade, was frustrated and coldly furious because of both. He knew deep down he had only himself to blame for having blown the whole business.

Everything had seemed to be going so smoothly two nights ago when he had led Jamie on board the yacht and down into the shadowy cabin. She had come with him, full of trust and a sweet, rather shy anticipation that had made him feel both infinitely protective and wildly victorious. The combination of emotions had been entirely new to him. They had formed a potent brew, singing through his bloodstream like a rare and exotic drug. The night had been magic. He had undressed Jamie so slowly and carefully, savoring the soft, rounded curves of her breasts and thighs.

There had been warm, gentle invitation in the depths of those wide gray-green eyes as he had slid the oversize glasses off her short, tip-tilted nose. The mass of dark auburn hair had tumbled tantalizingly around her shoulders when he'd pulled it free from the pins that held it in a casual swirl on top of her head. Cade remembered how he'd run his fingers through the rich stuff, delighting in the deep fire.

There was no overt classical beauty in her face, but the lively expressive features had caught and held him every time he'd looked at her during the past two months. She was twenty-nine years old and still suffering from what he considered a romanticized view of life and people. Cade had suspected she would probably never outgrow the charming touch of naïveté. He didn't mind. He found it somewhat amusing, even strangely pleasant to know that Jamie saw him through a rose-colored haze. It was a sure bet that few people had ever viewed him that way.

He'd known from the first day he'd walked into Fitzgerald's beautiful home that there would come a time when he would take Miss Isabel's intriguing employee to bed. But Cade had waited, willing to bide his time and do it right even though he was cognizant of her growing awareness of him. He'd liked her honesty in that regard. She hadn't played games. The initial shyness had been real but so had the initial attraction she'd felt for him.

For some reason it had seemed unduly important that the seduction of Jamie Garland be carried out carefully and properly. He still couldn't explain the way he'd handled that end of things. There had been no reason not to push matters much farther, much faster. But a part of him had insisted on taking his time and making everything perfect for her. And so the two months had drifted past in a haze of gathering sensual attraction and intellectual pleasure until they culminated quite naturally in an evening of exquisite passion. The only shadow on the horizon was that Cade knew he had to get her free of the Fitzgerald home before the authorities made their move.

Cade had thought his timing had been faultless. When he'd pushed her deeply into the cabin bunk and felt Jamie blaze with passion at his touch, he'd known she would follow him on board the yacht two days later. She would have done anything he'd asked of her. Glorying in her response to him, he'd lost himself in her that night. There had been a sense of wonder and power and warmth in taking Jamie Garland so completely. The two months of courtship had culminated in a night Cade knew he would never forget; a night that had left him starving for more even as it had satisfied him completely.

If all had gone well, the two of them would have been safely away from Santa Barbara by now. She wouldn't have been caught up in the scandal. The knowledge that everything had gone wrong instead had been eating at him for the past forty-eight hours and there wasn't much left of his self-control. Jamie's infuriatingly obstinate response to his attempts to explain the situation came close to making his temper snap completely. And something else was chewing on him; a sense of panic.

"Please go, Cade."

"Jamie, this mess with Fitzgerald has nothing to do with you and me."

"I'm not in the mood to appreciate your odd sense of humor."

"I'm not joking, damn it! I'm laying it on the line. We have a *relationship*, you and I."

"Is that what it's called?" she asked flippantly.

Cade sensed the high-strung emotions that were searing her nerves and knew he should back off for a while. Cade Santerre knew people. He had a talent for analyzing them and predicting their behavior. It was a skill he used almost unconsciously and it had often served him well. But although he knew intellectually what his course of action ought to be now, emotionally he wanted to force Jamie to understand and accept what had happened. He was afraid, Cade realized, afraid that she was going to slip through his fingers the way Fitzgerald had. But while losing Hadley Fitzgerald was annoying, after all the work that had been put into trapping the man, losing Jamie didn't even bear thinking about. She belonged with him now, Cade told himself for the hundredth time that day. They belonged together.

"I'm not interested in having any kind of relationship with you whatsoever," Jamie said stonily. Before Cade could reply the phone shrilled loudly. Automatically she turned to look at the white instrument where it sat on a glass-topped end table. "I suppose that's the press again. Why won't they just go away? Can't they get it through their thick heads I'm not going to talk to them?"

Cade released her and strode over to the ringing phone. "I'll handle it." He lifted the receiver and delivered a cold, unencouraging greeting. A familiar gruff voice responded. "Oh, it's you, Gallagher."

Jamie absently rubbed one shoulder where Cade's fingers had been unconsciously sinking deep into her skin and watched belligerently as Cade listened in unemotional silence.

"I see," Cade said finally, his eyes on Jamie. "No, I'm here; I'll tell her. You're absolutely sure it was Fitzgerald's boat?" There was another pause while he listened, and then he said a brusque goodbye and replaced the receiver.

Instantly on the alert, Jamie stared at him. "What is it? What's happened?"

Cade hesitated and then said coolly, "They finally located Hadley Fitzgerald's cabin cruiser. It's been missing from the marina since very early yesterday morning."

A quick frown brought Jamie's dark brows together. "His boat? Where was it?"

Cade sighed. "It was found drifting a couple of miles offshore. All indications are that Fitzgerald has committed suicide at sea."

Jamie's mouth fell open in stunned amazement. "Suicide!"

"Gallagher says that it looks like he must have thrown himself overboard," Cade concluded quietly.

"Oh, my God." Jamie's knees suddenly felt as if they wouldn't tolerate her weight. She dropped down onto the nearest chair, hugging her arms tightly to her breast. "Suicide. I never dreamed he was the type. I never thought...I just assumed he would lie low until he could prove his innocence. What will I tell Miss Isabel?"

Cade came toward her, crouching down beside her and reaching out to put a hand on her jeaned thigh. "I'll tell her for you, Jamie. You don't have to be the one. Let me handle it for you."

Jamie turned her head slowly to look at him. With great dignity she said very clearly, "Neither Miss Isabel nor I need any more bad news from you. You've done enough. Get out of here, Cade. I will be the one who tells Miss Isabel what's happened to her brother."

Cade read his complete and utter dismissal in her eyes and knew there was nothing more he could do in that moment. The sense of panic flared again. This time he dampened it with a hefty dose of logic. Time was what Jamie needed. She needed time to remember how good it had been between them these past two months. Time to reconsider his side of the story. Time to get over the shock of the events of the past two days. Time would be his ally. It would allow Jamie to regain her perspective, allow her to remember.

Even as he told himself all that, it occurred to Cade that time might provide something else.

There's just a chance, Cade realized, *that she might discover she's pregnant.* He was startled at the odd jolt of pleasure and possessiveness the thought gave him. If she were pregnant she would need him. She would have to come to him. And he would take care of her.

Cade got slowly to his feet and walked over to the end table that held the phone. Reaching for the note pad and the silver-plated pen that stood beside the telephone, he wrote quickly. Then he straightened and tore off the page.

"You can find me at this address, Jamie. If you need me for anything at all, or if you discover when you've calmed down that you don't want to throw away what we have going between us, look me up. I'll be waiting."

"You'll wait until hell freezes over," Jamie managed starkly.

"Jamie, honey, sometimes things happen..."

"Isn't it the truth!"

Cade reined in his sense of frustration and quieted the uneasiness he was feeling. He kept his voice gentle. "I meant sometimes our actions have certain, uh, ramifications. Unforeseen consequences..."

"Goodbye, Cade."

"Jamie, listen to me. If anything happens, anything at all, I want you to know I'll be waiting. Do you understand, honey? I'll be at that address. Waiting."

"Goodbye, Cade," she said again.

There was nothing more to be said. Cade left.

TWO

She must be pregnant.

Cade felt an odd twist of excitement somewhere deep inside. Satisfaction rippled through him next, and finally, incredible relief. It had been a long shot. After all, he had only been to bed with her once. But the timing fit, he thought with a sense of exultation. It fit perfectly.

After six weeks of alternating bouts of desperation countered by logical reassurance that he was doing the right thing by waiting, Cade realized he felt almost light-headed with relief. Determinedly he took control of his emotions. The last thing he wanted to do was to ruin everything now by mishandling the situation again.

He lounged in the stern of the oceangoing fishing boat he'd named *Loophole* in a rare moment of whimsy and watched as Jamie Garland walked hesitantly toward him. She held a scrap of paper in one hand and was glancing at the names of the boats tethered in the marina as she moved slowly along the bobbing, planked walk. In another couple of seconds she would spot the *Loophole*. When Cade had glanced up a few minutes ago and seen her poised in the sunlight at the gate of the marina, he had told himself very forcefully that he had been right to wait.

Six weeks. That was long enough for a woman to find out she was pregnant. At least he assumed it was. Cade's strong fingers closed fiercely around the can of beer from which he had been drinking. Six weeks. He had almost given up hope. The cold, clear-thinking side of his nature, the side that had always given him an instinctive ability to outmaneuver others, had insisted he wait as long as two months if necessary. It would all be so much easier if she came to him. And she would come to him eventually, he had assured himself over and over again. One way or another she would come to him.

At least that's what he had told himself during the long nights of the past six weeks when another side of him clamored for action on his part. The second aspect of his nature had surprised him at first with the extent of its power. Never had his emotions threatened to so completely overwhelm the logical, calculating elements of his personality. But during the past six weeks he had frequently found himself in the grip of a frustrated, raging male panic that almost convinced him he should ignore his intellect and go after Jamie.

Thank God he'd had the sense to maintain his self-control and wait for her. It would be much better this way. Jamie had obviously been forced to face the fact that she needed him, either because she had found herself pregnant or simply because she couldn't forget what they'd shared. Either reason, or a combination of both, suited Cade. He was, after all, a pragmatic man. He'd use whatever worked; whatever brought him the results he wanted. Pregnancy and passion were powerful forces in a woman. One or both of them was undoubtedly responsible for bringing Jamie to him at last. Given the proud, angry manner in which she had told him to get out of her life just a few weeks ago, he was inclined to lean toward the pregnancy theory. Nothing like finding out she was having a baby to make a woman reconsider her feminine pride, Cade decided with what he considered shrewd insight into the behavior of the female of the species.

He wasn't going to ruin everything now by letting her know he had dissected and analyzed her behavior. He'd play this cautiously. He wouldn't throw her pride back in her face. She'd admit the truth to him and to herself in her own good time. For now it was enough that she was here. Things were back on track. The sense of overwhelming relief turned into euphoria that had to be strictly controlled. Firmly he clamped down on his own reactions.

Cade took a long swallow from the can in his hand in an effort to steady himself. His fingers were trembling a little, he realized in wry disgust. The waiting was over, so why in hell was he succumbing to nerves? Ruthlessly he suppressed the sign of uncertainty. He watched Jamie's approach through eyes that were narrowed partially against the warm Southern California sunlight and partially in hungry assessment. It had been so long....

She looked wonderful coming toward him. The rich auburn hair was twisted into the familiar sweeping knot on top of her head. She wore her dark prescription lenses instead of the clear ones, and the frames were even more oversize and stylish. The white pants she wore were pleated and full at the waist, cropped at the ankles. A rakish, white linen shirt, open at the throat completed the outfit. Her bare feet were only minimally enclosed in a pair of thin-strapped sandals, and she carried the bulging, oversize shoulder bag she had toted everywhere during those two months in Santa Barbara. He'd teased her more than once about the large purse, but she'd only laughed and told him he ought to be grateful. It had carried more than one picnic to the beach.

Cade concentrated on her waist for a few seconds, wondering when a pregnant woman first began to show that fact to the world at large. Not this early, apparently. Of course, he reminded himself, there was always the possibility that she wasn't pregnant, but on the whole he was rather inclined to think that that reason fit the timing of her appearance best. Vaguely he understood that he wanted her pregnant because it gave him such a useful tie to hold her with. It was a tie she couldn't break. She was far too honest to deny him his fatherhood.

Jamie glanced once again at the name scrawled at the bottom of the slip of paper she held in her hand. The paper, containing the address of the marina in the little town just up the coast from San Diego, had become wrinkled and smudged during the past six weeks. She was lucky she had it at all, Jamie decided with a touch of irritation. She'd very nearly tossed it in the trash after Cade had walked out of the Fitzgerald home. She probably should have thrown it out. In fact, Jamie still wasn't sure why she hadn't discarded it and instead stuffed it unceremoniously into a zippered compartment of her purse. It had probably been sheer force of habit. She was so accustomed to tossing loose odds and ends into the bag that she'd added the scrap of paper without thinking about it.

But even as she reassured herself, Jamie knew she was lying. She hadn't kept the paper by accident. She might as well admit it.

The *Loophole* struck her as an odd name for a boat. She was quite certain it hadn't been the name of the elegant yacht Cade Santerre had used for two months in Santa Barbara. She was hardly likely to forget that particular boat. It had been called *Dreamer II*, and in her idiotically enchanted state of mind this past summer Jamie remembered thinking it was a lovely name for a beautiful craft on which dreams had become reality. The yacht had been brilliantly white, trimmed in rich teak. The cabin had been intricately outfitted, providing every luxury. There had been expensive wine in a small rack, pâté and caviar in the tiny refrigerator, and a stereo system stocked with classical music. And the view through the windows of the moon silvering the sea was one she would never forget.

She really was going to have to get control of this

unfortunate tendency she had to romanticize life, Jamie told herself brusquely.

She moved on to the next boat slip and almost walked right past the *Loophole*. The block letters painted in black and shadowed in red on the white stern of the large fishing boat registered just as she was about to walk toward the next slip. With a frown she glanced again at the name on the scrap of paper. A fishing boat? The last time she had seen Cade Santerre he had been the wealthy business-executive owner of a customized yacht.

"Hello, Jamie."

The dark husky tone brought Jamie's head up with a snap. She was suddenly very grateful she was wearing her sunglasses. At least they provided some semblance of concealment. For a long moment she simply stared at Cade as he leaned on the stern railing with the easy graceful nonchalance she recalled so vividly.

"Hello, Cade," she finally said slowly. He was wearing jeans that were faded from several washings, a cocoa colored short-sleeved shirt and a pair of rather worn-looking deck shoes that had been white once. The heavy leather belt that clasped his waist appeared to have been around even longer than the shoes. Cade had always dressed casually in Santa Barbara but the clothes he had worn there had been several times more expensive than the ones he had on now.

The harshly etched lines of his face and the tawny gold hunting eyes hadn't changed, Jamie thought. Nor had the sensation of quiet, controlled strength that emanated from Cade. He was watching her with an indefinable expression, an expression that made Jamie unexpectedly nervous. It was as if she had just walked into a trap he had set.

"It took you long enough to get here," Cade said gently. "Come aboard. I've got a couple of extra cans of beer." Suddenly his brows came together as though he had just recalled a stray fact. "Or are you supposed to have any alcohol? It seemed to me I remember reading something—"

"A beer," Jamie interrupted firmly, determined to take control of the situation right from the start, "sounds great." She decided to ignore the implication that somehow he had been expecting her, and his even odder reference to alcohol. She went aboard the *Loophole* with the knowledge that she must stay in charge.

"Have a seat, Jamie. I'll get the beer." Cade motioned her to a deck chair and disappeared for a moment into the forward cabin. When he returned he was holding two frosty, opened cans. Silently he handed one to her and then lifted his own in a too casual salute as he sank down into the seat across from her. His eyes never left her face.

Realizing that Cade wasn't going to say anything more to break the ice, Jamie drew a breath and asked the first obvious question that came to mind. "What happened to *Dreamer II*?"

"She wasn't mine. Belonged to a friend." Cade sipped his beer and waited.

Jamie nodded. "I always had a feeling she wasn't quite real." It was the truth. Nothing about the two months with Cade this past summer seemed real anymore.

"*Dreamer II* was real enough. She just doesn't happen to belong to me," Cade said roughly, as though he sensed Jamie's thoughts. "I needed her to make the right impression on Fitzgerald."

"I see." Jamie's mouth tightened as she lifted the can of beer to her lips. "I imagine that *Loophole* is a much more suitable name for a boat that belongs to you. A realistic, practical man would always have an escape route available, wouldn't he? You're hardly a dreamer, are you, Cade?"

Cade frowned. "Dreams aren't very useful things for a man. He needs clearer, more defined goals if he's going to get what he wants."

"You may be right," Jamie agreed thoughtfully. "The same theory would apply to women, too. You do have a talent for logic and decisive action, don't you, Cade? You were always so good at manipulating people and situations."

He didn't respond to the faint taunting in her voice. Instead, his own question was oddly quiet. "Have you been doing a little logical thinking yourself, Jamie? Is that why you're here?"

Jamie leaned back in her deck chair, wondering where to begin. "I'm not here because of any rational decision on my part. As a matter of fact, I voted not to come at all. Miss Isabel outvoted me. I'm here to carry out my employer's wishes." The lie came relatively easily to her lips. It should; she'd practiced it often during the drive down from Big Sur.

Cade's gaze pinned her abruptly. He appeared genuinely startled. "Miss Isabel sent you?"

"You seem disconcerted, Cade. Why did you think I'd tracked you down? Because I couldn't bear to live without you any longer?"

Sudden understanding seemed to flare in Cade's gleaming eyes. "Perhaps Miss Isabel knows what's best for you in this situation. She probably thought you'd be too proud to come looking for me unless she prodded you into it."

"She knows very well I didn't approve of this business of recontacting you." Irritably, aware that her present state of tension was making it difficult to think clearly, Jamie downed some more of the cold beer and got to her feet. She walked toward the bow of the boat, absently noting the neatly arranged array of gear. Assorted nets, fishing knives and tackle were all carefully stowed. She glanced into the front cabin.

"Jamie," Cade said, having risen silently to follow her. "Don't be afraid of me." He reached out to touch her hair. "I won't let you down."

Jamie stepped out from under his touch, conscious of the shock of awareness that had gone through her. She had to stay in control, she reminded herself yet again. Idly she pretended to examine some coils of rope that were lying neatly on the deck. "Quite a change from *Dreamer II*, isn't it? Do you really own this boat, Cade?"

"I own her," he replied softly. "I make my living with her. The *Loophole* is a charter boat. I take people deep-sea fishing."

Jamie shook her head in mild wonder. "I would never have guessed this past summer that you made a living as a charter-boat captain. You certainly had me fooled. I believed, along with everyone else, that you were a successful, wealthy executive. Amazing. Absolutely amazing."

Cade stepped closer, his expression suddenly dark and intense in the bright sunlight. "Are you shocked, Jamie? I told myself this summer that when you found out what I really did for a living, it wouldn't matter to you."

"It doesn't," she assured him, swinging around to confront him fully. She managed a lightly defiant smile. "Makes no difference to me at all as long as you're still for hire."

Long lashes briefly concealed the tawny gold eyes, but not before Jamie was certain she had seen a flash of grim astonishment in his gaze.

"For hire?" Cade asked carefully. "What does that mean?"

"It's very simple," Jamie said coolly, sitting back down and picking up her can of beer. "Miss Isabel has instructed me to hire you."

Cade looked momentarily blank. "Hire me to do what? Fulfill my responsibilities to you? She can't possibly believe she'd have to pay me to do that!"

It was Jamie's turn to look blank. "What responsibilities? You don't owe me anything, Cade. We both know that. We shared a brief affair this past summer and now it's over. I'm here to talk business."

He gave her a wary glance as he resumed his own

seat. "Maybe you'd better start at the beginning. Where is Miss Isabel, by the way?"

"We took your suggestion. I put her on a three-month cruise. She left two weeks ago."

Cade nodded. "It will be good for her. How did she take the news about her brother's suicide?"

Jamie had the distinct impression he was asking out of genuine concern, but she discounted the notion. Cade wasn't the type to become overly concerned about his victims.

"About the way you'd expect. She was shattered at first."

Cade shook his head. "I suppose that's not surprising. She adored him. I doubt that she would ever have believed him guilty of the tax-shelter fraud. You should have let me tell her about the suicide, Jamie. I know it must have been hard on you."

"It was," she said simply. "But I think it was easier coming from me than from the man who had pulled the rug out from under her beloved brother."

Cade's expression didn't change. He continued to look at her levelly. "You can forget the little barbs and taunts, honey. I don't feel guilty for what I did and nothing you say is going to make me feel responsible for Fitzgerald's death."

"You just did what you had to do, hmm?" Jamie allowed nothing but cool sarcasm to show in her tone. She refused to let him see the fragility of her self-control. "Nothing like genuine machismo to fall back on when the ethical side of things gets complicated."

"I think," Cade observed far too politely, "that we

are straying from the subject. Let's go back to Miss Isabel's request to hire me."

"Ah, yes. Miss Isabel. I think you did your best work on her, Cade. She has great faith in you, in spite of everything. Or perhaps because of everything."

"Do you want to clarify that?" Cade asked patiently.

Jamie looked at him narrowly. "Miss Isabel, to put it succinctly, does not believe her brother committed suicide. She wants you to find out what happened to him. She seems to feel that because you investigated him so thoroughly in the first place, you probably have more of an idea of how to find him than anyone else possibly could. I have to agree with her, Cade. You're a thorough man. You probably know just about everything there is to know about Hadley Fitzgerald's way of operating."

"His way of operating?" Cade repeated. "That sounds as though you may believe he was a little less than innocent."

Jamie stirred uneasily, inwardly annoyed at her slip of the tongue. "The authorities seem to have found a great deal of evidence against him," she admitted austerely.

"He was guilty as hell."

Anger flared in Jamie. "I'm not here to discuss his guilt or innocence. I'm here to ask you if you'd like another investigative job. A simple 'yes' or 'no' will do."

Cade gave her an unexpectedly affectionate smile. "Are you quite certain that's why you're here, Jamie?"

"Of course I'm certain!"

"Are you sure it's the only reason?" he prodded softly.

"What other reason could there possibly be?" she challenged.

"You don't have to fake it, honey. Not with me." He put out a hand and captured one of hers. "We got very close this past summer, you and I. I know a lot about you."

"Such as?"

His mouth curved in gentle amusement and he moved the pad of his thumb across the fragile veins of her wrist. "Such as the fact that you don't lie well."

"Unlike you?" she couldn't resist saying recklessly.

His fingers closed around her wrist. "I know you've got your pride, Jamie, but I think you've had your pound of flesh. There's no need to go on hurling accusations."

Her mouth firmed as she met his eyes unwaveringly. "You're right. I'm not here to sling more accusations at you. It would be a pointless exercise, wouldn't it?"

"I told you I know you very well, Jamie Garland. And I knew you'd be showing up sooner or later."

"Your arrogance is rather charming in a way," she told him. "Somewhat outrageous and somewhat amusing, I suppose." Jamie pulled her hand free from his grasp and was surprised when he allowed her to escape. "But I don't have time to play games with you. I'm here to offer you a job. Take it or leave it."

Cade drummed his fingers absently on the arm of

his chair while he studied her intently. "I thought Miss Isabel was out of the country."

"She is. She'd like you to work on finding her brother while she's gone. If you turn up anything, I can reach her by contacting her cruise ship. I have complete instructions on how to do so."

"You're serious, aren't you?"

"Miss Isabel's serious," Jamie corrected calmly. "I, personally, advised against hiring you for the job." White lies, Jamie assured herself, mercly white lies. After all, in the end Miss Isabel had agreed to the idea.

"You're claiming you're just here to carry out her orders?"

"Since she was gracious enough not to fire me after that debacle six weeks ago, I figure carrying out her orders is the least I can do," Jamie snapped.

Cade scowled. "You're still viewing what happened between us as a disaster?"

"I'm trying to learn how to be realistic, just like you."

Cade's expression softened. "Such sweet bravado. Charming. A little outrageous and rather amusing, I suppose," he added with a small grin as he threw her own words back at her. "But totally unnecessary. You're here and that's all that counts. If you want to pretend it's because you're offering me a job, go ahead. I don't mind."

"I am not pretending! That's exactly why I am here. Now do you want the work or not?" Jamie glanced around meaningfully. "Perhaps your charter work doesn't leave you any time to accept this sort of assignment right now?"

"Don't sound so hopeful," he said dryly. "I can make the time. The part about finding out what happened to Fitzgerald is for real? Miss Isabel really wants me to look into it?"

"Yes."

"It does make a convenient excuse," Cade said, nodding thoughtfully.

"It's not an excuse," Jamie exploded tightly.

"Whatever you say, honey."

"Damn it, Cade, if you're not going to take the job seriously, then forget it."

"After Miss Isabel's gone to all this trouble to provide you with a way of approaching me that doesn't hurt your pride? I wouldn't dream of it. I accept the offer of employment." Cade took a long swallow of beer and grinned at Jamie's infuriated expression. "Did she happen to say how much she's paying?"

"I'm empowered to negotiate your fee. Miss Isabel assumed it would be quite high," Jamie said stiffly.

"Miss Isabel is a very astute woman."

"Well?" Jamie demanded, as calmly as she could. "How much?"

"For finding out whether or not Fitzgerald might still be alive? I'll have to think about it. I'll let you know over dinner tonight."

Jamie brushed aside the reference to dinner. "Why do you have to think about your fee? Don't you have an established amount? How much did you get paid for your work this summer?"

"You don't seem to understand exactly what it is I do for a living," he retorted smoothly. "I'm not a private investigator. I'm a charter-boat captain. There's a difference."

"But someone hired you to go after Hadley Fitzgerald in the first place," Jamie pointed out. "I remember you said something about your relatives having invested in one of his, uh, programs." She had almost tripped over the word 'scheme'. Something in her did not want to grant this man the satisfaction of knowing that she suspected he had been right about Hadley. She had already surrendered too much to Cade Santerre.

"My sister and her husband didn't hire me to do the job. They simply asked for some advice. They were desperate. I started looking into the situation and decided I might be able to put a stop to Fitzgerald's activities. Then I got in touch with the authorities, who already had a lot of questions and suspicions. We put together an operation designed to find Fitzgerald's real set of accounts, not the one available for public inspection at the L.A. office."

"And you found them at his home in Santa Barbara. With my help," Jamie tacked on disgustedly.

"I would have found them with or without your help. Jamie, we've been through this. You're a fool if you're feeling guilty. You have absolutely no reason to feel that way. Fitzgerald deserved to be exposed and you know it. You're too genuine and honest yourself to condone criminal behavior. Would you actually want to let someone like Fitzgerald continue operating just because you worked for his sister, who happened to be a nice old lady?"

"Now you're the one straying from the main subject," she retorted haughtily. "About your fee—"

"I've told you, I'll decide and let you know over dinner," Cade said with an air of finality. "Where are you staying?"

Jamie frowned. "At a little motel in town." She gave him the name.

"I know it. I'll pick you up around six."

"I don't think dinner is necessary!"

"Come on, Jamie," he coaxed with unexpected gentleness. "What about just for old times' sake?"

"When I think of the 'old times' we spent together, I have a tendency to lose my appetite."

"I'll pick you up at six," Cade repeated with a new touch of cold steel in his voice.

Jamie took one look at the chill in the tawny gold eyes and knew she couldn't win; not if she wanted to carry out Miss Isabel's wishes. Putting down her can of beer with unnecessary force, she acquiesced with a short nod and made her way off the *Loophole* without a backward glance.

Cade watched her leave, disconcerted by the abrupt departure. Whatever her real reasons for seeking him out, there was no doubt that her pride was still at full sail. She was just tense, he told himself. Maybe a little scared. She was clinging to Miss Isabel's plan to hire him as though it were the real reason she was here. But under the surface, Cade was sure he had seen the warm, vulnerable woman who had fallen so sweetly into his hands this summer. The Jamie Garland he had seduced so carefully and had come to know so intimately was still there under that protective veneer. She was just a bit frightened at the moment.

Tonight, after some good wine and reassuring conversation he would bring her back to the *Loophole* and recover what had been his this past summer. The difficult part was over. Jamie had come looking for him. He had told himself firmly that it was crucial she take the first major step. But now she'd done it and he could take over. The thought of seducing Jamie again awakened a throbbing heat in his veins that he'd had to keep bottled up for six long weeks.

Cade went to work, sharpening a knife he frequently used for filleting his clients' catch, unaware of his own smile of satisfaction. He looked forward to undoing the last of Jamie's fears this evening. It was good to be able to take action again. The waiting had been almost intolerable. A man could become a nervous wreck waiting for a woman to come to her senses.

Several hours later, seated across from him at dinner, Jamie was intensely aware of Cade's smile. In fact, she decided wryly, the anticipation and satisfaction in Cade was evident in far more than the cool, pleased curve of his mouth. The two blatantly masculine emotions pervaded his fascinating eyes and lent a husky quality to his dark voice. And they reminded her far too much of the past summer.

"Excellent fish," she remarked, valiantly attempting to keep the conversation on an impersonal level. The comment was valid. Her broiled swordfish had been cooked to perfection. The Caesar salad and crusty sourdough bread that accompanied it made a perfect combination. But she would have said the same words even if the food had been lousy. She was experiencing a real need for casual, remote dinner-table conversation.

She had made every effort to maintain a detached, impersonal image this evening. The dress she had chosen was a sophisticated red wrap affair belted with a wide, black leather sash. The ensemble had seemed suitable for a business dinner. Her hair was in its usual casual twist, but that was largely because she couldn't think of anything else to do with it. She had deliberately not put on one of the dinner dresses she'd worn in Santa Barbara.

"The place is noted for its seafood," Cade told her easily. "But I chose it because it reminds me a little of that restaurant we used to go to so often in Santa Barbara. Remember? The one that looked out over the marina?"

"Vaguely," she replied unencouragingly. Actually she recalled every evening there with unsettling clarity. Cade had behaved then as he was behaving tonight; solicitous, rather possessive, deeply, intently aware of her. It was that attitude of total awareness that had seduced her so conveniently once before, she reminded herself. She must be wary of it now. "It seems to me you wore that jacket a time or two in Santa Barbara. I take it you didn't have to return it when you returned the yacht?"

Cade registered the faintly derisive words with a slightly raised brow and then shrugged beneath the fabric of the expensively tailored linen jacket. "I have a few clothes left over from the days when I did other things for a living besides run a charter service."

"What did you do for a living before getting into charter work?" Jamie asked. "Something that made your relatives think you could get them out of the trouble they'd gotten into by investing in Hadley's programs?"

"Something like that," he verified dryly. "I was an accountant."

"An accountant!" For some reason that startled her.

"Had my own firm in Los Angeles. If there's one thing a good accountant knows how to do, it's to dig for information relating to money."

"How big was this firm?"

"Big enough. Does it matter now? I sold out to some of my employees a couple of years ago and I don't have any intention of going back into that line of work."

Aware of the strength of the willpower that seemed to underlie the decision, Jamie grew curious. Curiosity was a dangerous element to introduce into the casual, remote pose she was attempting to maintain, but she couldn't seem to control it. "You acted the role of successful executive very well this summer. I take it, it's because you once were one?"

"Would it make any difference to you tonight if I still were the man I posed as this summer?" he asked. He was watching her intently.

"I don't know," she said honestly. "At least it would be one less thing you'd lied about."

His expression hardened briefly and then turned cool and analytical. "You're really determined to push me tonight, aren't you? Be careful, honey. I'm willing to tolerate a certain amount of feminine vengeance from you, but there are limits."

"What will you do if I make one too many nasty cracks? Quit working for Miss Isabel? That's not a very effective threat, Cade. I advised her not to hire you in the first place. And if it's true that your background is in accounting, not investigative work, then perhaps she really should try someone else. I think she was under the impression that you were a professional criminal investigator."

"Believe me, if Fitzgerald is alive, I'll have a better chance of finding him than a regular private eye would. A man like Hadley has a distinctive way of operating. The technique he uses to handle money, locate potential clients and set up scams is as unique to him as a fingerprint is to a burglar. If he's out there, I can find him sooner or later. He won't be able to resist getting right back to work. But frankly, I doubt he's still around. No one has turned up any evidence to contradict the impression that he took his boat out to sea and decided not to come back."

"Miss Isabel is convinced he's still alive," Jamie said with a sigh.

"Miss Isabel is trying to avoid having to face reality."

"You're real big on that, aren't you?" Jamie

snapped. "Did you face reality when you decided to quit managing your own accounting firm and become a charter-boat captain? That sounds like a rather ridiculously romantic move to me. Come on, admit it. You had some wildly romantic view of making your living from the sea instead of a sterile office, right?"

Cade smiled faintly. "No. I sold my firm because I woke up one morning and realized that I didn't like being responsible for fifty employees and a lot of tense clients. Building up the business had been exciting. Running it was not. I needed a whole new career, and I knew that if I stayed with the firm I would eventually grow bored and burn out. So I made a logical decision to start over in an entirely unrelated line of work."

Jamie looked at him in faint astonishment. He really believed what he was saying. Perhaps he had made such a dramatic decision based purely on a logical assessment of his own needs, but deep down she wondered. A man who made love the way Cade had that night on the yacht must have a streak of passion and romance in him somewhere. Or was she only telling herself that because deep down she couldn't bring herself to believe he was completely devoid of that kind of emotion? She was more the fool for romanticizing him! There could easily have been another reason why he'd changed careers so drastically. Maybe the accounting business had failed. Perhaps he'd run it into the ground. But even as she speculated on that possibility, Jamie knew it wasn't very likely. Whatever Cade Santerre did, he would do well. The odds were strongly against him having a real romantic streak in his soul. On the other hand, the only thing you could call her scheme to contact Cade again was romantic, unless you wanted to label it stupid.

"We haven't yet discussed your fee," Jamie said firmly, determined to bring the conversation back in line. "Have you settled on a figure?"

"We can discuss it later," he replied carelessly. "Right now we're talking about personal job histories and I've got a few questions about yours."

"You do?"

"Hmm." Cade buttered a chunk of bread. "Are you going to stay with Miss Isabel indefinitely?"

"She pays me well and I like her very much. It's a good job so, yes, I suppose I will stay as long as she's willing to have me work for her. Besides, where else is someone who graduated with a degree in history going to find such a well-paying position that offers so much travel and variety? I get to make my home base at her beautiful house in the mountains of Big Sur up in northern California. I get to travel with her frequently when she takes vacations as she did this summer when she went to stay with Hadley. And she treats me almost as if I were her daughter. I did hear that the CIA occasionally hires liberal-arts types and it does offer travel, but other than that outfit, I don't think there's too much out there for people with my background," Jamie said lightly.

"I doubt that. I saw the variety of duties you handled for Miss Isabel this summer. There were a lot of skills involved and I'm sure you could easily market those skills elsewhere. You did just about everything for her," Cade recalled slowly. "You took care of her business affairs, her taxes, her clients, her entertaining."

"Miss Isabel likes to devote herself entirely to creating new works of art. She doesn't care to be bothered with the business side of life. She depends on me completely in those areas."

"And you, in turn, are suitably faithful, loyal and obedient, is that it?"

"It's a living," Jamie shot back coolly.

"I wasn't mocking you, Jamie," Cade said softly. "In fact, I admire your loyalty to Miss Isabel. But there comes a time in everyone's life when you have to think about going in new directions, making changes. You shouldn't feel completely tied to Miss Isabel. Working for her is, after all, only a job."

Confused at the way the conversation was going, Jamie stared at Cade. "What are you getting at?"

He hesitated, sorting out his words and then said, "It's just that this past summer and now tonight, when you describe your job I have the impression that maybe you're a little too devoted to dear Miss Isabel."

Cold resentment caused Jamie's eyes to narrow behind the lenses of her glasses. "There was a time when I seriously considered walking away from dear Miss Isabel and running off with a man who wanted to sail into the sunset. Fortunately reality intruded."

"And instead you went running right back to the security of working for Miss Isabel."

"There is nothing wrong with working for her! Or are you going to accuse her of being somehow involved with her brother's schemes?" Jamie demanded furiously. "If she is, then so am I, because I handle all of Miss Isabel's business affairs!"

Cade cut through the emotional outburst. "Calm down, Jamie. I never meant to imply any such thing. I was only pointing out that you're not obliged to stay with Miss Isabel forever simply because you feel guilty for what happened six weeks ago. You should feel free to move on when, uh, circumstances dictate a change in your life." He seemed to stumble over the last few words as if he weren't certain how to express himself.

"Circumstances have not yet dictated a change. As it turns out, I'm damn grateful for the job. It might have been a little hard to get another after that scandal six weeks ago!"

"Don't let your feelings of loyalty toward Miss Isabel govern all your actions," Cade went on harshly. "There are more important kinds of loyalty you should be concerned about other than the kind you feel toward Miss Isabel."

"Such as?" she challenged rashly.

"Such as the loyalty you owe to your lover," Cade declared bluntly. "The loyalty you owe to me. You've had six weeks to think about it, Jamie. But you're here now and that means that on some level, at least, you've realized that this is where you belong. I like Miss Isabel, and if you want the truth, I suspect she invented this little job of finding out what happened to her brother largely to give you an excuse to come down here and find me. But I'm willing to go through with it and see if I can verify the suicide if it will make her rest easier about her brother's fate. Afterward, though, I'm not going to continue to share you with her. She needs someone virtually living with her and you won't be able to do that because you'll be living with me."

THREE

"You're serious, aren't you?" The last forkful of tender swordfish halted halfway to Jamie's mouth as she stared at her escort in stunned amazement. "You're really serious. I can't believe it."

"Can't believe what? That I want you? I never made any secret of that. I told you six weeks ago that our relationship had nothing to do with getting Fitzgerald."

"Just an unfortunate coincidence, I suppose? I had no idea I appeared so incredibly naive. Look, Cade, I think this has gone far enough. Obviously Miss Isabel's plan to hire you is not going to work out. I think you'd better take me back to the motel." Jamie realized she had crumpled the napkin in her lap into a sorry state. With great care she made an attempt to smooth it out and refold it. It was difficult to keep her fingers from trembling. She was getting cold feet, she realized with a sense of anxiety. The knowledge angered her. Determinedly she gathered her willpower.

"Jamie, just relax, will you?" Cade invited in a low, reassuring murmur. "I'm not going to rush you. I know you need a little more time. But you've taken the first step. Trust me to handle the rest. I gave you plenty of time this summer, didn't I? All the time you needed."

All the time she'd needed to fall in love, Jamie thought bleakly. And when he'd sensed she was in the palm of his hand, he had shown her the full extent of her own passion for him. Oh, yes, he'd given her time. And enough rope to hang herself.

"I told Miss Isabel this was going to be a disaster. Will you please take me back to the motel, Cade?" It took a tremendous effort but Jamie was proud of herself for the control she exerted. Deliberately she placed her napkin on the table beside her plate, signaling her readiness to depart. She had to make it appear that she didn't care one way or the other if he accepted the job. She had to be cool and detached. It was the only manner in which she could stay in charge. It was crucially important to stay in control. Any other direction would only lead to disaster.

"Back down, Jamie. No one's going to push you. I don't want you getting upset. You know it's not good for you." Cade threw her a half annoyed, half concerned glare as the waiter hurried toward them.

The odd comment about not getting upset raised a few questions in Jamie's mind, but she brushed them aside as Cade asked for the bill. Her main goal at the moment was to conclude this evening, which, she had known from the outset, was going to be difficult.

In silence the dinner check was settled, and in silence Jamie allowed herself to be escorted out into the parking lot where Cade's black Mazda sports car waited. Jamie wondered what had happened to the expensive Mercedes-Benz he had driven this summer. Perhaps it had been returned to its rightful owner along with the yacht. It was difficult to know what had been real and what had been fiction about Cade Santerre during those two months in Santa Barbara. It was safest for her to assume that nothing had been as it seemed. Jamie had been telling herself that, morning, noon and night for the past six weeks. She didn't dare stop the litany now.

Jamie took refuge in the night-darkened interior of the car but she was fiercely aware of Cade's aggressive, controlled presence beside her. Whatever else had been accomplished this evening, at least she had managed to erase some of the pleased satisfaction from his smile. Unfortunately she wasn't sure she liked whatever it was that had replaced it. The silence as he drove began to wear on her nerves. She had a hunch he knew that and was deliberately letting the condition continue. One of the lessons she had learned this past summer was that Cade had an instinctive ability to manipulate people. When she could stand the subtle pressure no longer she struggled for a neutral topic.

"About Miss Isabel's job..."

"I've said I'll look into the situation for her," Cade reminded her stonily.

Jamie slid him a speculative glance, but other than the implacable set of his features in the darkness she could detect little. Then she decided to risk saying what must be said. "If you do decide to take her offer of employment, it must be with the understanding that I don't come with the deal."

Silence descended again as Cade failed to respond to the warning. Jamie could think of nothing else to say until she finally realized they were pulling into the parking lot of the marina. Belatedly she became alert to her surroundings.

"This isn't the motel, Cade."

"Since you don't seem to be abstaining from alcohol, I thought I'd invite you in for a nightcap," he replied too easily as he switched off the ignition. "Remember how pleasant it was to go back to the boat after dinner in Santa Barbara and have a glass of brandy?"

Jamie remembered very well. Fleeting images of nights spent under the influence of warm brandies, sea-scented air and Cade's gradually deepening embraces would stay with her the rest of her life. A brief wave of panic washed over Jamie before she regained control of herself. She knew what he was doing. He was trying to invoke the magic that they had shared those two months in Santa Barbara.

"It won't work, Cade, but I guess there's no harm in letting you see that for yourself." With a blitheness she didn't quite feel, Jamie stepped out of the car as Cade opened the door.

"We'll see, honey." He smiled down at her and then linked his fingers with hers as he started toward the marina gate. "Just relax and let things flow naturally. Everything's going to be all right."

For the first time genuine humor lightened Jamie's mood. "For a confirmed realist, you're doing an absolutely amazing job of deluding yourself, Cade Santerre."

"Am I?" But he didn't seem worried. The anticipation and satisfaction were again very evident in him. The small setback he had experienced during dinner no longer seemed to be troubling Cade.

"Yes, but perhaps after you've had a dose of reality we can settle down and do business together."

He grinned at her and tightened his grip on her hand. "You're not the one to teach me about reality, sweetheart. You're much too soft and gentle and trusting."

"I don't trust you!"

"A temporary state of affairs." He paused beside the *Loophole* and gallantly assisted her on board, his smile still faint and teasing. "After you. It's not exactly *Dreamer II* but it's home."

She looked at him in surprise. "You live on board?"

"Yes. Very convenient."

"Well, considering it's a fishing boat, I'm surprised the, uh, odor of fish isn't stronger."

"You know me, Jamie. I keep things clean and neat."

"Yes, you always were a thorough sort of man."

He led her down the steps of the forward cabin and waved her to a seat on the bunk. Then he opened a cupboard and brought out a bottle of brandy.

"I see your tastes are still expensive in some respects," Jamie noted dryly as she caught a glimpse of the label.

"I don't compromise on the important things." He handed her a snifter and toasted her lightly. "To Miss Isabel." Then he set down the glass and casually removed his coat and loosened his tie.

It was all very unthreatening on the surface. Just a man relaxing after a dinner out. But somehow the atmosphere in the small cabin began to vibrate with subtle masculine sensuality.

Jamie blinked and lifted her glass. "I can drink to that. I don't believe in compromising, either."

She glanced around the tidy, cramped quarters of the cabin. There was one bunk, a small galley and a great deal of cleverly designed cupboard space. Fine for a few days at sea, she decided, but hard to imagine living in on a permanent basis. She wondered what the exact state of Cade's income was. Somehow the idea of him not really being wealthy didn't reassure her as it should have. She ought to be feeling less intimidated by a man who was closer to her own income bracket. The brandy warmed her and she leaned back against the bulkhead just as Cade sat down beside her.

"Where are you staying while Miss Isabel is on her cruise?"

"At her house near Big Sur."

"I'm surprised she didn't want you to accompany her on the cruise."

Jamie shrugged. "She said the cruise was supposed to be therapy, not a genuine vacation. She didn't want to take me along and end up depressing me for three months. Besides, there's a lot to do at home."

Cade frowned. "Home? You're talking about her place in Big Sur?"

Jamie swirled the brandy at the bottom of her glass. "It's become my home during the two years that I've been working for her. I'll leave the phone number with you so that you'll be able to contact me if you learn anything about Hadley's fate."

Cade sipped his brandy and looked at her over the rim of the glass. "It will be easier if I work out of Miss Isabel's house."

Jamie's head came up in surprise. "But you have a business to run here."

"I have a friend who can take the boat out when there's a scheduled trip," he returned carelessly.

"Cade," she began firmly, "I don't see any need for you to move into Miss Isabel's home." That was the last thing she could allow, she decided in a brief flare of panic. She had to keep a careful distance between herself and Cade until she'd discovered whether or not there was any real hope of picking up the pieces of her love.

"I could do the job from here but it makes more sense to work there. I assume Miss Isabel will have all kinds of odd information about her brother available. Photos of him on vacation, for instance. He might have retreated to one of those spots again if he actually faked his suicide. A man like Fitzgerald would choose a familiar place in which to hide out because he doesn't like dealing with new environments. That was one of the characteristics that made it easy to track his activities. He tended to stay in a limited geographical area and operate in a certain, recognizable manner. A man doesn't generally change his fundamental way of doing things any more than he has to in order to survive. Especially a man of Fitzgerald's age and temperament."

"You seem to understand him very well," Jamie breathed, a little frightened by the cool, undoubtedly accurate assessment. Whatever else had changed about Cade, he was still a very logical, calculating man.

"I'm usually fairly good at analyzing the motives and actions of others," he said with unconscious arrogance.

"And at manipulating them?"

"One talent usually leads to the other." He set down his brandy glass and reached for the one in her hand. Gently he removed it and put it down beside his own. "Don't be afraid of my limited skills, honey. They're all I have to use against your magic."

Her senses shivered in warning, but Jamie didn't protest as Cade drew her slowly toward him. This moment had to be faced and conquered, she told herself bravely. She had known that from the instant she had decided to take the chance of contacting Cade. There was no way beyond proving to the man she had loved that he could no longer control her as easily as he had this summer. It wasn't just Cade who needed to realize that, Jamie thought bleakly. She needed to be certain of it, too. She would be living in a state of constant tension until she had faced the sensual questions and dealt with them.

"There's no magic, Cade," she whispered as he slid his hands gently around her throat and tilted her face upward. It was a soft, husky protest, uttered with desperate conviction because she could feel the tendrils of the sorcery she feared.

"There is always going to be magic between us." He brought his mouth down on hers, brushing her lips lightly, persuasively.

Jamie could feel the leashed control he was exerting and momentarily wondered at it. It seemed to her that he was having to use a great deal of strength to keep from overwhelming her defenses with sheer masculine aggression. The very fact that he was making the effort intrigued her. Did he want her so very much?

"Jamie, Jamie, I've missed you so. It's been hell waiting for you." Cade's thumbs moved in slow, luxurious circles just below her ears. The small caress was infinitely erotic. "Did you know what you were doing to me by making me wait so long?" He spoke the words against her mouth. "Do you know how many times I've lain awake remembering that last night we had together?"

"No, Cade," Jamie managed, as despairingly she recognized that on one level, at least, he was right. The physical magic they generated between them was still strong. "I don't know the answer to any of your questions." *That's why I'm here,* she added silently; *to discover the truth about you and me.*

"The answers don't matter now that you're here.

I've wanted you so badly, sweetheart," he groaned, leaning backward and drawing her down on top of his chest.

Just for a moment, Jamie promised herself. She would allow her senses to be engulfed once more for only a moment. She barely felt it when he slipped the glasses off her nose. The strong hands, so excitingly familiar to her from six long weeks of unwelcome dreams, began to move on her body. Jamie knew she shuddered beneath the touch and was aware that Cade knew it also. A distant voice of warning reminded her that he was a man who would use such information. He had a talent for manipulation.

"Don't be afraid of me, Jamie. I only want to make love to you once again. I need you, honey. God, how I need you. Don't you remember how good it was that night?"

The passionate seductive words flowed over her, dark and coaxing. Jamie closed her eyes, knowing she had to put a stop to this soon or she was lost. She needed time, carefully structured and controlled time before she took this chance again.

Cade's blunt fingers traced the line of her throat to her shoulder and then followed the V-shaped collar of the red wrap dress down to the lowest point. The dress had seemed demure enough when Jamie had put it on this evening, but the feel of Cade's touch as he explored just under the edge of the fabric was electric. It was as if she were wearing only a nightgown meant to be discarded.

No man had ever had the effect on her that Cade

did, and she knew that he probably realized it. The longing to touch him more intimately took control for a moment and Jamie's trembling fingers toyed with the buttons of his white shirt.

"Go ahead, sweetheart," he urged thickly.

She found herself obeying. A little awkwardly she undid the buttons, telling herself at each step along the way that she had to stop soon.

"Cade," she whispered achingly as her copper-colored nails laced through the curling hair on his chest. "Oh, Cade..."

"I think you've missed me a little, too," he murmured in satisfaction. Deliberately he let his palm slide across the fullness of her breast. Beneath the fabric of the dress he felt the added protection of the bra she had worn. It was a very well designed, very prim little bra made of rather sturdy, plain material. It was not a romantic scrap of lace and satin of the sort she had worn during the two months in Santa Barbara. "You didn't need all this armor just to go out to dinner with me, honey." He chuckled affectionately. "Did you think I was going to assault you?"

Something clicked in Jamie's head. "No, Cade. That's not your way, is it? You don't assault. You infiltrate and manipulate. You're a very devious man. I must be sure to remember that." She lifted her head to look down at him. Without the aid of her glasses his features weren't as clear as they might have been, but she had no trouble distinguishing the flare of displeasure that appeared in the tawny eyes.

"Jamie, hush. You don't know what you're saying."

"Oh, yes, I do, Cade. I know exactly what I'm saying. And I know what I'm doing." Taking a deep breath and a firm grip on her wayward emotions, Jamie pushed herself free of the treacherous embrace. She didn't know where she got the strength to summon up the cool little smile, but it came from somewhere. She reached casually across Cade to pluck her glasses off the shelf where he had put them. Then she glanced meaningfully at her watch. "My goodness, how did it get so late? Time I was going. Thanks for dinner and the brandy, Cade. Miss Isabel will be pleased to know you're going to accept her job offer. I'll send her a message when I get back to Big Sur."

"Now wait just a minute, Jamie. Where the hell do you think you're going?" He sat up quickly as she slipped off the bunk.

"Back to the motel, of course. Where else?" She glanced at him over her shoulder, gray-green eyes reflecting only mild surprise that he should have to ask the question. "Don't worry about driving me. I can walk from here. It's only a few blocks."

"You'll walk back to that motel over my dead body."

"Don't tempt me."

"Jamie, come back here. You don't want to spend the night alone in that motel and you know it. Why the devil are you being so obstinate? You're the one who came looking for me!" Shirt still unbuttoned and hanging loose, Cade got to his feet, confronting her in the narrow confines of the cabin.

Well aware of the domineering, intimidating threat

of him, Jamie called on her inner nerve and stood her ground. His cool, questioning smile never wavered. "You seem to be under some trite romantic misconception about why I came looking for you. Amusing, isn't it? This past summer, I was the one who tended to romanticize events. Now the shoe appears to be on the other foot. Be careful, Cade. It gets tricky trying to view the world through a pink haze. Everything gets distorted. A word to the wise."

Cade glowered at her, clearly torn between anger and uncertainty. The conflict mirrored in his eyes only lasted for a few seconds, but that it should have been evident for even that length of time startled Jamie. Perhaps he wasn't as sure of her as he'd like her to believe.

"All right, lady. You want your revenge. I guess I can't deny you that much. Just don't push it too far, okay?" He took her arm and propelled her forcefully out on deck. "It's been a long six weeks, honey."

"Cade, I think you're leaving imprints in my arm," she pointed out tartly as he hustled her along the walk between the tethered boats. She didn't know whether to be relieved or alarmed at his change of mood.

"I'd like to be leaving a few imprints elsewhere on your anatomy. I would never have guessed this summer that you could be such a stubborn little creature."

"Maybe you didn't get to know me quite as well as you thought you did," she risked boldly as he stuffed her unceremoniously but not ungently into the passenger seat of the Mazda.

For a split second the tawny gold eyes gleamed in

the glow of the parking-lot lights. During that brief moment of fierce tension Jamie forced herself to remember that Cade Santerre was a dangerous man.

"I know you very well, Jamie Garland. Don't you ever forget it."

Several pithy responses to that statement went through Jamie's head as they sped back toward the motel, but none of them seemed likely to give her the last word so she kept her mouth shut. A flash of common sense warned her that she was lucky to be ending the evening this coolly and decisively as it was. There was no point in tempting fate.

In the motel parking lot Jamie jumped out of the Mazda before Cade had even switched off the ignition.

"An evening with you is always interesting, Cade. Thanks for dinner. If you decide to go ahead with Miss Isabel's little project, even though I'm not part of the fee, you can reach me at this number." She delved into her huge bag and handed him one of Miss Isabel's cards with the address and phone number of the house in Big Sur on it.

Cade was out of the car, reaching to take her arm before she could escape into the motel lobby. He took the card and shoved it into his pocket without looking at it. "We'll talk about the details of this in the morning. I'll pick you up for breakfast."

Wisely Jamie didn't argue. "What time?" she asked demurely.

"Is seven too early?" He was making an obvious attempt at recovering some semblance of politeness.

"No. Seven will be fine."

"Jamie, there's no need to run from me tonight," he said quietly as they came to the lobby door.

"I would prefer to keep our relationship on a businesslike footing, Cade. You shouldn't have any trouble with that. After all, you managed to court me for two months this past summer without once forgetting your real business in Santa Barbara. I have every confidence that you can keep your mind on your work."

He shook his head in wry disbelief. "You're determined to make both of us suffer before you admit the truth, aren't you?"

"What truth?"

His powerful hands moved soothingly on her upper arms as he faced her in the shadowy light. "That you're here because you need me."

"I've admitted Miss Isabel needs you, or thinks she does."

"*You* need me, Jamie. I know it must have been difficult for you to come back to me, honey. But it was inevitable. One way or another we were bound to be together again. I knew if I just gave you some time you would realize that what we shared this summer wasn't a casual affair."

"It seemed quite casual to me," she remarked with forced brightness. It was infuriating to know that he'd been right in many ways. When he'd made no effort to contact her during the past six weeks, Jamie had known she couldn't stay away from him.

His temper flared briefly. "If it had been really casual, I would have taken you to bed the first night I took you out to dinner! It would have been easy enough to do. You were ready to fall into my hands from the moment we met. Maybe that was where I made my mistake. If I hadn't been so concerned with doing things properly, I wouldn't be standing here tonight having this ridiculous argument in front of a motel."

"Sleeping with me for two solid months and then letting me find out you'd been using me to trap Hadley wouldn't have endeared you to me any more than did sleeping with me for one night and letting me find out the truth. What I can't figure out is why you still think you can have your cake and eat it, too. If you need Miss Isabel's job, then do the work. You'll be paid. But don't think you can pull the same stunt you did this summer. A check for services rendered is all you'll be receiving. For the last time, Cade, I am not part of the deal." Whirling, Jamie slipped through the sliding glass doors and into the motel lobby. She was gone in an instant, disappearing up the staircase to her room on the second floor.

The night clerk watched her go and then glanced curiously at Cade standing outside in the darkness. For an instant the clerk's eyes met Cade's in an ancient male expression of commiseration and then he shrugged and went back to the magazine he'd been reading. Cade could almost read the other man's mind. *Win a few, lose a few.*

Except that he hadn't lost yet, Cade told himself forcefully as he stalked back to the Mazda. And after waiting this long, he sure as hell didn't intend to lose at all. Things had gotten a little rocky at times this evening, and the night hadn't concluded quite the way he'd planned, but progress had been made. She was here and she had accepted a dinner invitation. Afterward she had almost let herself be persuaded back into his bed. He'd come so close to having it all again. It had been a near thing. If he'd just kept his mouth shut at the appropriate moment, she wouldn't have taken fright. Next time he would be more cautious. He'd botched things this evening somehow and the knowledge annoyed him. What was the matter with him, anyway, he demanded in silent self-chastisement. Where was his normal finesse?

Cade slammed the key into the Mazda and yanked the car into gear. Next time matters would end properly. And after that it would be clear sailing. Because once Jamie had surrendered again, there would be no going back. He was done with waiting.

"Dance while you can, lady," he muttered as he sent the Mazda hurtling forward into the darkness. "Time is running out for you. The ball ends at midnight, in case you've forgotten." He might not be Prince Charming, Cade acknowledged grimly, but he was the one the lady would find waiting when she finally accepted her fate.

It was late in the afternoon the following day when Jamie decided she'd better stop for groceries before driving the last fifty miles into the dramatic Big Sur country of northern California. The lonely highway ahead hugged the side of the mountains as the Santa Lucia Range swept down to meet the surging Pacific

Ocean. It was a spectacularly scenic trip, but the region was very unpopulated. The few stores she would encounter during the last portion of her drive existed primarily to serve campers, and most would be closed by the time she reached them.

The fog was already gathering out at sea, Jamie noticed as she pulled into the parking lot of a small convenience store. She wanted to be home before it cloaked the land. The narrow highway that she would be following for the next several miles was precarious in places. Not a road to be driven in fog.

It had been a long, tiring trip. Jamie stifled a small groan as she climbed a little stiffly out of Miss Isabel's tomato-red Audi. She had left the motel at six-thirty that morning, praying earnestly that Cade would not decide to pick her up early for breakfast. But there had been no sign of him as she'd checked out and tossed her suitcase into the car. She turned left as she'd pulled out of the motel parking lot, deliberately avoiding the route out of town that would have taken her past the marina. The last thing she had wanted was to meet Cade coming the other way.

It had been quite easy to get up early, pack and leave well ahead of the seven o'clock deadline. After all, she hadn't been able to sleep well, anyway. She was half annoyed and half proud of the way she had handled the situation into which she'd so unwisely catapulted herself. Jamie winced as images of moths and flames came to mind.

The decision to tentatively, *cautiously* confront Cade again had been a reckless one, and Jamie knew it, but she had been unable to keep herself from doing it. Talking Miss Isabel into hiring him to search for her brother had been a way of providing protective cover for herself, but she wasn't sure it would work. The man she loved was shrewd and dangerous, and she hadn't been completely certain of her camouflage. But this time around, she'd vowed, she would be the one in control. She would not play the role of ripe peach again.

His utter confidence in his ability to rekindle the fires of their relationship was probably the only factor that had saved her from making a complete fool of herself last night, Jamie decided as she walked into the little store that adjoined a gas station. Never let it be said that pride couldn't give a woman fortitude. Who did he think he was to take the attitude that all he'd had to do was wait for her to come to him? The fact that he had been partially right was galling. She pushed the knowledge aside.

Brows drawn together in a severe little frown, Jamie selected some low-fat milk, cereal and a few vegetables. The small assortment of items, together with the supply of canned and frozen goods at the house, would tide her over for a few days. She could always drive into Carmel in a day or two if she ran out of anything. It was fun to spend time in the self-consciously quaint little town by the sea.

As she deliberated between whole-wheat bread and rye, she found herself once again asking the question that had been plaguing her since the previous evening. When all was said and done, why should Cade show such a strong intention to renew the relationship? She had, after all, dismissed him very haughtily from her life.

She understood her own actions. She knew what had driven her to seek him out. She was obviously a woman who loved unwisely but completely. Jamie was not, however, certain about what motivated Cade.

He had only been using her during those two months this past summer. There had been no words of undying love from him that night on *Dreamer II*. Nothing to indicate he had suddenly fallen head over heels in love with her. He hadn't claimed he couldn't live without her. In fact, he hadn't claimed as much last night, she thought ruefully as she decided on the whole-wheat bread. Cade had misled her, even used her in some ways, but to give the devil his due, he hadn't lied to her about something as important as his own feelings for her. He had wanted her this past summer and apparently he still wanted her, but he hadn't claimed to love her.

She ought to be grateful for finding some element of honesty in him, Jamie decided wrathfully as she carried the small basket over to the checkout counter. After all, a woman liked to know that the man to whom she had given her heart had a couple of good points in his character!

At least she had made a strong start at reclaiming her pride, if not her heart, last night.

"Will that be all?" the high-school boy behind the counter asked disinterestedly as he began totaling up the contents of Jamie's basket. It was obvious the youth was not viewing his after-school job as a stepping stone toward a career in the retail business. He appeared quite bored.

"That's it for the groceries. I'll need some gas, though."

"It's self-service. Help yourself. You pay my dad next door."

Automatically Jamie glanced out the window at the stand of gas pumps that adjoined the convenience store. A nondescript dark Buick stood waiting for its owner to finish paying for fuel. As soon as the Buick was driven off, she could pull the Audi into position. Jamie hated pumping her own gas. On the other hand, she hated paying the extra few cents per gallon that it cost to refuel at a full service station. Ah, well, she'd be home soon, and she could tolerate the smell of gasoline on her hands until then, she supposed.

She was about to refocus her attention on her groceries, when something about the silver head of the man who had just finished paying for his gas caught her attention. His back was toward her as he climbed into the Buick, but there was a familiarity about him that caused her to try to get a good look at his face. There was no chance. The man slammed the door of the Buick and set the car in motion, without once glancing sideways or back over his shoulder.

Jamie stood staring out at the car as it pulled onto Highway 1 and headed north. The man had been in his late fifties, she estimated, with a well-styled wealth of aristocratically gray hair.

"Eight ninety-five, ma'am," the clerk said in a prompting tone.

"What?" Confused by the incredible thought that had struck her as she watched the man in the Buick, Jamie belatedly pulled her attention back to the business of paying for her groceries. "Sorry, I was thinking about something else." Quickly she dug out a ten and waited for change.

Silver hair. Somewhere in his fifties. A certain, familiar dignity in his bearing. If only she'd gotten a better look.

Jamie shook her head impatiently as she hurried out to the waiting Audi. She was letting her imagination, or perhaps Miss Isabel's imagination, run away with her. It wasn't possible that she'd really seen Hadley Fitzgerald. She had simply seen someone who reminded her of him.

As much as she hated to give Cade Santerre credit, she had to admit that he was undoubtedly right in arguing that Fitzgerald had died at sea. The authorities who had investigated the incident had agreed. Jamie decided that she had spent too much time listening to Miss Isabel trying to pretend her brother was still alive. The poor woman had simply not wanted to accept the truth. And because she was so fond of her employer, Jamie had found herself occasionally beginning to doubt the facts. Well, it was only fair enough, she supposed. After all, it was Miss Isabel's belief that her brother was still alive that had given Jamie the excuse she needed to seek out Cade.

* * *

"What the hell do you mean, she checked out half an hour ago?" Cade roared at the startled desk clerk. "She was supposed to be ready for breakfast at seven o'clock!"

"I'm sorry, Mr. Santerre," the middle-aged woman said for the tenth time. She was clearly affronted. "She said nothing about having an appointment with you. She simply paid her bill and left. Said she had a long drive ahead of her."

Cade leaned forward, both large hands spread flat on the desk. "That means she's headed for Big Sur."

The woman backed up a step, uncertain of the temperament of this man who was practically accusing her of aiding and abetting Jamie Garland's escape. "Possibly, Mr. Santerre. Yes, quite possibly she's headed home. A, uh, logical destination, I imagine."

"That house in Big Sur isn't her *home*," Cade growled dangerously. "It's her office. Her place of employment. She doesn't have a real home of her own."

"Oh."

"She thinks it's charming and adventurous and rather romantic to work for an eccentric artist and live in a picturesque place like Big Sur."

"Well, it does sound kind of interesting," the woman said placatingly, clearly having no idea at all about the subject at hand. "I mean, isn't it close to Carmel? Such a lovely little town, Carmel."

Cade showed his teeth in a smile that would have done justice to a wolf. "It is not charming or adventurous or romantic to me. As far as I am concerned, it is not even interesting. Her job has become a damned nuisance, in fact! It would have made things a lot simpler if Miss Isabel had fired her six weeks ago."

"Miss Isabel?" the clerk inquired warily.

"If Miss Isabel had fired her, Jamie wouldn't be suffering from a case of excessive, misplaced loyalty. Nor would Jamie have had someone to shelter her for the past six weeks. She wouldn't have had any place to run this morning. She would have been forced to accept the fact that she needs me and that deep down she wants me."

"I see." The clerk nodded very cautiously.

With an abrupt restless movement Cade straightened and turned toward the door. "Why am I standing here yelling at you?"

"I was wondering the same thing myself."

Cade didn't hear the muttered answer to his rhetorical question. He was already halfway out to the parking lot. The little idiot had flown the coop. More evidence than ever that she must be pregnant. He'd always heard pregnant women tended to be high-strung and occasionally irrational. It seemed to him that he remembered his brother-in-law complaining, albeit good-naturedly, about Meg's moods when their first child was due last year.

Then again, it wasn't strictly accurate to call Jamie the idiot. He was the fool for letting her get away last night. He should have taken a firmer stand with her, overwhelmed her sensually, shown her that he could crush any defense she had raised against him.

But he hadn't thought it necessary to push her that hard. He'd been under the impression that the battle had been won already. After all, she'd come looking for him, hadn't she? That trumped-up excuse about checking into Fitzgerald's death was clearly just that: an excuse.

Cade wrenched open the Mazda door and slid inside. It was perfectly possible that Miss Isabel did, indeed, want some confirmation of her brother's death, but she was an intelligent woman. She had been aware of the rapidly intensifying relationship growing between her personal assistant and Cade Santerre during the summer. She was not above playing matchmaker.

It was obvious now to Cade why Miss Isabel had resorted to creating this "job." The woman had probably been as startled as Cade had been by Jamie's streak of feminine pride. Jamie had always seemed so sweet-tempered, so gentle and understanding. Spirited but amenable. Good-natured. Cade had been certain that after the shock of discovering his true business in Santa Barbara, she would forgive and understand.

Apparently, finding out that she was pregnant had stirred up a surprisingly primitive streak of vengefulness. She seemed very much inclined to make him run in circles for a while before she surrendered again, Cade decided in gathering irritation. She wanted revenge.

But she couldn't play games for long. Being pregnant put her on a strict timetable.

Even so, Cade knew, he was no longer willing to wait out her moods. He'd already cooled his heels for six weeks and that was long enough. She'd taken the first step, and he had no intention of letting her retreat.

Cade drove back to the marina to pack his bag and make a few phone calls. It was a long drive up to Big Sur.

FOUR

Jamie turned the key in the door of Miss Isabel's home with a vast sense of relief. The fog had been thickening rapidly along the coastal highway, and she was lucky to have finished the trip without having to deal with the worst of it. It was creeping inland swiftly and would soon blanket the cheerfully bizarre structure Jamie and Miss Isabel termed "home."

Jamie remembered liking the house on sight when she had arrived for her interview two years ago. It seemed exactly the sort of place in which a brilliant, eccentric artist ought to live. Clinging precariously to the edge of the heavily wooded mountain, it had a distant view of the crashing Pacific, seen through a primeval forest. Miss Isabel had proudly explained that the house had been designed and constructed by members of a local commune that had flourished briefly during the late sixties and early seventies. The earnest young men and women who had been experimenting with an alternative life-style on the edge of the Pacific had long since left the mountains to become stockbrokers and lawyers. But while they had lived their dream in Big Sur, they had applied their creativity to house design. The results were original, to say the least.

Fashioned of timber and glass, the structure consisted of a variety of oddly shaped rooms, none of them conventionally square or rectangular. Some were domed, some faceted, some pie-shaped and some simply strange. All of them had fantastic views and all of them were filled with the overflow of Miss Isabel's labor. When working, the older woman was driven by a tremendous energy that resulted in an incredible quantity of art.

"Why don't you sell some of these, Miss Isabel?" Jamie had asked after she had been working for her new employer for a month. "You've got a fortune in your own work hanging on the walls."

Miss Isabel had grimaced and then proceeded to explain the facts of an artist's life. "If I put too much out on the market, it would bring the prices down on all my work. Simple economics, my dear. The law of supply and demand. Too much product and the demand goes down. When the demand goes down, the prices drop. Keep the supply limited and people fight to get an Isabel Fitzgerald work. And the prices stay high."

"But in the meantime you're stuck with lots of extra paintings and ceramics because you can't stop working, can you?" Jamie had nodded perceptively. She was quickly coming to realize that her employer was not quite as scatterbrained and eccentric as she appeared on the surface. Isabel Fitzgerald was a very smart woman. Smart enough to maintain a healthy balance between business and art.

"Unfortunately, when the mood is on me, all I can do is go into the studio and work," Isabel had said with a sigh. "So the stuff piles up. That's one of the reasons I bought this place. It's big enough to hold it all."

Jamie's own room was filled with a selection that Miss Isabel had allowed her to choose from the vast array of art hanging on walls or sitting on tables throughout the house. As she walked into the unabashedly exotic art deco bedroom, Jamie felt her customary sense of pleasure. The room was octagonally shaped, with every other facet of the eight-sided wall sheathed in painted mirrors. The designs on the glass were flowing ornamental trees that had come straight from the depths of Miss Isabel's imagination during a period when she had become fascinated with glass painting. A flamboyantly graceful and rather erotic ceramic figure of a nude female stood on the round black lacquer table beside the bed. A huge beautiful cloisonné jar stood on an end table near the pillowed window seat. The carpet was a thick plush patterned in swirls of ivory, and the bed was covered in burgundy.

It had been home to Jamie for two years, and as she unpacked she told herself she was infinitely grateful to be back. The thought of risking another evening in Cade Santerre's vicinity was enough to send a nervous chill down her spine. She had gotten lucky last night, but that kind of luck didn't last. From the first time she had met him Jamie had been aware of a sense of inevitability about her relationship with Cade. A part of her had known from the start that sooner or later she was fated to wind up in his arms. Fate had accomplished its goal this past summer. She would be a fool to give it another opportunity without first asserting herself as his equal, not some easily manipulated little fluff-headed female.

She needed to let Cade know she was not the brainless creature who had dropped into his palm like a ripe peach. This time around she would set the terms of the relationship, or there would be no relationship.

But the sense of relief at temporarily having escaped was tempered with a strange, wistful sadness that hovered at the edges of her awareness as she finished unpacking and went into the kitchen to find something to eat. In spite of the end result, Cade had brought something unique into her life. She had undoubtedly fallen heedlessly in love with the wrong man, and there was no doubt at all that she had taken a great risk by contacting him again. The idea had seemed much more workable when she'd been occupied with Miss Isabel's problems, but now Miss Isabel was several thousand miles away. The house seemed empty and the idea no longer seemed so workable.

Puttering around the sleek black-and-white tiled kitchen, Jamie fixed herself a salad and opened a bottle of an interesting Sauvignon Blanc. She deserved the glass of wine, she decided as she dug out a corkscrew. She wondered how Cade had reacted this morning when he'd learned she had left town. She hoped the kindly-looking desk clerk hadn't had to bear the brunt of Santerre's displeasure.

The cork was half out of the bottle when she heard the car in the driveway. Jamie hesitated for a moment in surprise. Unbidden, a faint trickle of uneasiness pervaded her bloodstream. This was ridiculous, she thought. Probably a result of that fleeting glimpse of a man who had vaguely reminded her of Hadley Fitzgerald. Determinedly she finished removing the cork, set it down on the counter and went toward the front door. If there was a nondescript Buick parked in the drive, she was going to be very nervous indeed, she decided ruefully.

It was a black Mazda that was occupying the space beside the Audi. Tendrils of fog ebbed and swirled around it as the driver cut the lights and opened the door. It was no nondescript Buick, but there was no doubt about whose car it was.

"This," Jamie gritted through her teeth, "is what comes of getting involved with a thorough, tenacious sort of male." She flung open the door and stood on the threshold, jeaned legs spread apart, her hands on her hips. Seething, she glowered at the solid, lean figure coming toward her through the damp fog and shadows. "What the devil do you think you're doing following me like this, Cade?"

"There's nothing like a sweet-tongued, loving woman waiting at the end of a long trip," he observed laconically as he strode forward with a leather flight bag slung over his shoulder. "Good evening, Jamie.

Have a nice drive? You forgot something this morning."

"Like what?" she challenged.

"Like breakfast. We were supposed to have it together, remember?"

"It must have slipped my mind."

"So I'll take dinner instead." He came to a halt directly in front of her and bent his head to drop a short, hard kiss on her startled mouth. Then, without waiting for a response, he pushed past her into the curving living room. "What a crazy place. Looks just like something you'd choose in which to live. I'll bet you think it's delightfully artsy and wonderfully eccentric."

"It is."

"The hell it is. Looks like a bunch of hippies designed it back in the sixties."

"Nobody asked your opinion!"

He stood for a moment examining the room, which was designed in a half circle. The curving portion was comprised of floor-to-ceiling windows and during the daytime provided a dramatic view of mountain and sea. It had been furnished in wicker and bamboo to create a romantically tropical look. Several of Miss Isabel's collages provided eye-stopping counterpoints to the charming serenity of the room.

Cade shook his head in mild disgust and dropped the leather flight bag on the sisal matting that covered the floor. He swung around to face his unwilling hostess. "I suppose you have a good explanation for sneaking off this morning?"

Jamie used the excuse of shutting the door to avoid

the brooding examination of those tawny eyes. He wasn't supposed to be here, she thought on a note of hysteria. He was supposed to stay down south while she manipulated the contact between them. Everything was going wrong. "A perfectly good explanation. I felt like leaving, so I did."

"Nervous after last night?"

"You can stop looking so damn smug. No, I was not nervous after last night. I simply decided we had nothing more to say to each other until you have a progress report for Miss Isabel." Jamie stalked past him into the kitchen and headed for the counter where she had left the wine. "Don't tell me you've got news already!" Yanking a glass from the cupboard, she splashed wine into it and turned to face him. She peered wrathfully at him through the lenses of her glasses. "But, then, you always were a fast worker."

"Not fast enough, apparently. Give me a glass of that stuff. I need it. That's a hell of a drive on a night like this."

"Good thing you've had some recent practice," she shot back. "It will help you when you get back in the car in a few minutes and start toward Carmel. I do think Carmel is your best bet. You'll stand a much better chance of finding a motel there than you will if you go back toward San Simeon."

He came forward and poured his own glass of wine when Jamie made no effort to oblige. "Nice try, honey, but you know it's not going to work. I'm staying here tonight. Nobody but a complete idiot would attempt to drive that road in this fog."

"Since you just drove it, what does that make you?"

His mouth twisted in self-mockery as he raised his glass. "A very annoyed, very irritated idiot. Wise young women do not try to provoke such creatures. What's for dinner? I'm starving."

"Do you really think you can just land on my doorstep and announce you're staying the night?" Jamie demanded, outraged.

"It's not your doorstep," he pointed out far too politely. "It's Miss Isabel's. And I am currently working for Miss Isabel. That gives me a few privileges."

"According to whom?"

"Me. Jamie, for your own sake, I'm warning you not to give me any more trouble today. I've about had it. I was not in a good mood this morning when I discovered you'd taken to your heels. That state of mind has not improved in the past several hundred miles of driving. I'm tired and I'm hungry and I badly need this drink. If you display half the intelligence I credited you with this summer, you will close your mouth and fix me some dinner. What's that you're eating?"

"Salad," she grumbled, aware that the advice she was receiving was probably sound. Cade was definitely in a temperamental mood at the moment, and instinct warned her to tread warily. Damn it, she wanted him to be the one who had to tread carefully. She wanted to be the one to stipulate the terms of this arrangement.

"Is that all you've got?"

"There's some canned soup and the makings for some sandwiches," she grudgingly acknowledged.

"Fix us both some. You should be eating more than a salad."

Blankly, Jamie looked at him. "Why?"

He frowned. "Because you need to eat properly at a time like this."

"What are you? A nutritionist? I'll admit I'm under some stress at the moment, but I don't think a salad will hurt me."

"We can discuss proper diet over a proper meal. Which room is mine? I'll put my bag in it."

"Now wait a minute, Cade."

"Shall I find one for myself?"

Knowing she was fighting a losing battle, Jamie surrendered with bad grace. "There are only two bedrooms made up, mine and Miss Isabel's. I suppose you'd better take mine. I'll move into Miss Isabel's room." Setting the wineglass down on the tile counter with an angry snap, Jamie whirled to lead the way.

Behind her Cade paced along the curving hallways, staring at the wealth of artwork.

"Good Lord, I had no idea Miss Isabel was so prolific."

"She holds a lot of her work off the market," Jamie muttered.

"Of course. The last thing she'd want to do is flood the galleries. It would ruin her image, not to mention her income."

At the door of her bedroom Jamie turned her head to glance at him in mild astonishment. "That's exactly what she told me. Law of supply and demand. How did you know?"

"I used to be an accountant, remember?"

"Oh, yes, I remember. An *investigative* accountant." She nodded derisively as she walked into the bedroom. "I'll collect a few of my things and take them into Miss Isabel's room. Honestly, Cade, I don't know why you had to show up like this. There was absolutely no point in trailing after me."

"No?" He examined his surroundings. "Are you sure you weren't expecting me, Jamie? I have a hunch I'm playing right into your hands." He tossed the bag down onto the bed before meeting Jamie's shocked eyes. His own gaze mocked her with both indulgence and irritation. "Come on, honey. We both know you're trying to salvage a little of your pride. After all, you had to swallow a big chunk of it to come looking for me in the first place. I'm trying to be generous, but it's beginning to wear on my temper. Does it give you a certain amount of satisfaction to know I came chasing after you on such short notice?"

"Not particularly!" Jamie exploded.

"That's too bad, because you're probably not going to get a whole lot more in the way of revenge. I don't like games. Time is running out for you, honey."

"Believe me, I have no intention of playing games with you!" Infuriated, Jamie wrenched open a few drawers and removed a supply of underwear, and a nightgown as well. Without another word she stomped out of the room and went across the hall into Miss Isabel's oddly angled bedroom.

The first thing that greeted her as she flipped on the light was the portrait of Hadley that Miss Isabel had finished shortly before she had consented to leave on the cruise.

"Oh, Hadley," Jamie muttered to herself, "a great deal of this is your fault. If it hadn't been for you, I wouldn't be in this mess."

Miss Isabel had worked in her usual frenzy to finish the picture of her brother. The painting was a modernistic combination of collage and heavily daubed acrylics that resulted in a full-length, haunting portrait of Hadley Fitzgerald. The work of art had gone directly into Miss Isabel's bedroom the moment it had been completed, and Jamie had privately decided that it had been her employer's way of coming to terms with her brother's fate. Jamie hadn't had a good look at it at the time it was finished and hadn't wanted to press Miss Isabel on the subject.

Now she saw that while Hadley's features were quite clear and finely drawn, the rest of the canvas contained some bizarre elements. A dollar bill had been lacquered in among the brilliant daubs of acrylic paint, along with a portion of a letter to one of Hadley's clients. All over the canvas there were bits and pieces of objects that Jamie guessed represented Hadley's life and business. Even a broken pencil had been attached in one corner, together with a sheet from an account book. Jamie studied the portrait for a moment and then turned away. She had more important matters to handle. There would be time enough later to scrutinize Miss Isabel's most recent creation.

"Miss Isabel is a fan of minimalism?"

Jamie glared at Cade, who had walked across the

hall to stand in the doorway. He ran a quick eye over the spare, clean lines of the white-on-white room.

"I guess you could say that." She threw her underwear into an empty drawer in the white lacquer and stainless steel dresser.

"Your room, on the other hand, is a romantic, exotic hideaway, for you, isn't it?" Cade smiled for the first time since he had arrived. "But you can't hide in it any longer, sweetheart."

"Cade..." she began with a sudden ache in her voice. "What did you think you could accomplish by following me like this?"

"Let's go eat," he said easily. "I really am starving."

Three hours later Jamie climbed into the white-covered bed, which had been placed right in the middle of the strangely angled room. She lay staring at the ceiling and wondered whether she was seriously misleading herself by thinking that she had maintained control of the potentially volcanic situation this evening.

She had not been in control of anything this past summer, and it was probably folly to tell herself that things were different this time around. Yet it seemed to her that although he was being unbelievably persistent all of a sudden, Cade was also exhibiting a streak of caution. He had chewed her out for leaving without notice this morning, but he implied he understood her actions. He had settled down on a sofa with his feet propped up on an old sea chest and eaten his meal beside her in relative good humor. Jamie had been suspicious.

"There really is no way you can stay, Cade. You'll have to leave in the morning," she had said quite firmly at several points during the evening.

"Miss Isabel is my employer, not you. And she's not around to evict me, is she?" Cade had answered with a smile.

"What is it you want from me?" Jamie had demanded, beginning to feel desperate.

"You know the answer to that." His smile deepened with alarming persuasion. "I've missed you during the past six weeks, honey."

"If you had really wanted me in the first place, you wouldn't have used me to get Hadley this summer. And if you had really missed me, you wouldn't have spent the past six weeks lounging around on that boat of yours," she'd eventually shot back rashly. "You would have spent the time trying to apologize and explain your actions!"

He'd appeared momentarily taken aback. Then he'd given her a long, considering look. "I thought it would be better if you took the first step."

"Another of your theories on how to manipulate and control people? Cade, I didn't come crawling back to you. In case you haven't noticed, I contacted you for strictly business reasons."

"Honey, I never wanted you to come crawling back. I just wanted you to realize that what we had together was good. Too good to throw away because of anger and pride."

"Well, I sought you out on business. Nothing else is involved. I want that to be quite clear, Cade."

He'd only smiled again with that oddly indulgent curve of his mouth that contained so much quiet sureness and satisfaction. Jamie had finally excused herself and stalked off to bed. There was no dealing with the man that night. He was in the house and she was stuck with him until she could figure out a way to get rid of him.

But if he thought she'd looked him up because she wanted to throw herself back into his arms, he was out of his arrogant male head, she vowed as she lay in the darkness of Miss Isabel's room. Apparently he hadn't paid any attention to the lesson she'd tried to teach him last night when she'd coolly ended the sensual scene on the boat's bunk and gone back to the motel.

Except she hadn't been that cool about it at all, she admitted with a small sigh. A primitive restlessness had kept her awake for a good portion of the night following her dramatic little scene. There was no denying that a strong, deeply feminine part of her would have rejoiced in another act of love. She had never stopped wanting Cade, even though there were times when she thought she hated him. Fortunately, Jamie told herself firmly, she was in control of that portion of her psyche these days. The new relationship with Cade would be governed by her brains, not her emotions. The latter had ruled her long enough this summer. With that assurance, she eventually slipped into sleep.

She didn't know what it was that awakened her a long time later: perhaps the sound of rain on the windows; perhaps just the fact that she was sleeping in someone else's bed instead of her own.

Whatever it was, it brought her to drowsy wakefulness. She stirred and rolled over onto her side. And quite suddenly her heart began to pound.

The portrait of Hadley Fitzgerald had come alive.

Jamie's breath caught in her throat. *I don't have my glasses on*, she thought in panic. *That's all it is. I just can't see properly. It's an optical illusion.*

Hadley's silvered head moved slightly. The whole portrait seemed to shift, and for an instant Jamie could have sworn there were two images of Hadley Fitzgerald.

More frightened than she could ever remember being in her life, Jamie nevertheless fought for self-control. It must be her eyes. She needed her glasses. Squeezing her lashes shut for several seconds, Jamie frantically willed the effects of the double vision to disappear. Then, still keeping her eyes closed, she reached out to grope for the glasses she had left on the cylindrical night table.

A new wave of heart-stopping panic washed over her as her fingers brushed across the surface of the table and failed to make contact with the chic designer frames. Her lashes flew open as her pulse raced into high gear. *Where are my glasses?*

Dreading what her improperly focused eyes would see, Jamie jerked her gaze back to the portrait that stood in the shadows. Only one gray-haired image seemed to be staring at her from the darkness now, thank heaven. But she couldn't be sure. She couldn't be sure of anything at the moment. The urge to scream was almost overpowering. Jamie wasn't sure how she controlled it.

Getting out of the room seemed of paramount importance suddenly. Glasses or no glasses, she had to get away from the nightmare her sleepy brain had conjured.

Shoving aside the covers with an act of will that seemed tremendous, in fact, almost more than she could manage, Jamie struggled out of bed. Her bare feet found the white carpet and then she was running toward the closed door of the bedroom. Reaching it, she pulled it open and darted out into the hall without glancing back over her shoulder. The door closed rather loudly behind her.

Ridiculous to let the nightmare affect her this way. As soon as she was safe in the hall, Jamie began lecturing herself. Absolutely ridiculous. She stood there in the expensive, unabashedly sexy French nightgown she had bought last summer when she had begun to realize she was in love and told herself she was acting like an idiot.

She was still standing there, willing her pulse to calm down, when the door across the hall opened and Cade materialized. For some reason her uncorrected vision had no trouble with the details of his image.

He stood there wearing only a pair of briefs, his dark hair slightly tousled from the pillow, sleek shoulders looming powerfully in the shadows. He should have looked dangerous, but instead the sight of him offered great comfort.

"At least," she noted quite carefully, "there aren't two of you."

"Just as well. I wouldn't be willing to share you. Come on in, Jamie. I've been waiting for you."

The dark, persuasive words soothed and beckoned, promising warmth and passion in place of irrational fear. As if in a trance, Jamie took a step toward Cade. "I had a bad dream," she whispered.

"Did you? Come here, honey, and I'll help you forget all about it."

Jamie drew a long, steadying breath. She was awake. She knew what she was doing. "Silly of me to overreact. Haven't done that since I was a kid."

Cade's teeth gleamed for a moment in the darkness, and she heard the trace of masculine amusement in his voice. "You don't need any excuses to come to me, sweetheart." He held out his strong square hand. "But if it makes it easier for you, by all means use them."

She trembled, but not with fear. Slowly she put out her own hand and let his fingers swallow hers. Instantly she was caught and held. Cade drew her closer. "It's not an excuse, Cade. I really did have a nightmare." His nearness was extraordinarily comforting, she realized.

"You won't have any nightmares in my bed," he promised huskily as he tugged her gently forward. "I'll make certain all your dreams are very pleasant."

The elegant French nightgown whispered encouragingly around her ankles as Jamie allowed herself to be drawn into the shadows of the bedroom. She felt as though she were drifting, floating, gliding. Like a beautiful sailing yacht upon a warm tropical sea. Her senses were spinning.

"You'll assume too much...." she managed awkwardly, trying to put her uncertainties into words. "You'll think everything is settled; that you have it all back under control."

"Does it matter?" he whispered, closing the bedroom door behind her.

"Probably," she said softly. "It will be harder than ever to convince you that I'm not the same ripe plum I was this past summer."

"When I have you nestled in the palm of my hand again, you could probably convince me of just about anything," he said whimsically.

"You don't understand, Cade," she began earnestly.

He cut off the hint of urgency in her tone by sealing her mouth with his own. With a tremulous sigh, Jamie accepted the inevitable. Just as she had known this summer that the affair with Cade would end in bed, she knew tonight that there was no point trying to resist the pull he had on her senses. Cade was instantly aware of the surrender.

"Jamie, Jamie, you won't regret it. Here in my arms is where you were meant to be. We both know it." The words were murmured achingly against her lips as Cade's blunt fingers found the delicate fastenings of the French nightgown.

"It will be different this time, Cade," she tried to warn. Her senses were already responding to the magic in his touch as he slipped the gown off her shoulders.

"Better. It will be better this time."

"You don't understand…"

"Hush, sweetheart. I understand everything. You don't have to explain a thing," he soothed. "And you don't have to worry about a thing, either. I'll take care of you. You can trust me. Just the way you trusted me this summer. I'll make everything all right again. I promise."

The gown slid to her feet, and Cade groaned as he let his palms glide from Jamie's shoulders to the budding peaks of her breasts.

"Oh, Cade," she whispered as desire unfurled within her.

"How could you ever pretend to yourself that there wasn't real magic between us?" he asked thickly.

"I don't know," she admitted simply and lifted her arms to wrap them around his neck.

"Jamie!"

She was locked against him, her breasts crushed tantalizingly against the hardness of his chest. Cade's hand flattened along her back, sliding down to the full curve of her hips. There his fingers sank erotically into the soft resilient flesh. Cade's body reacted fiercely, and Jamie took deep, feminine pleasure in the knowledge. He was right. There was magic between them. Why should she deny it or herself? This time, she vowed, she would stay in control.

"I've been going crazy for the past six weeks!" With an abrupt, decisive movement, Cade lifted her high into his arms and carried her across the room to the bed. "This time you're not going to run out on me. I'd lose my mind if you did."

Jamie felt herself lowered to the sheets, and then she lifted her lashes to watch as Cade stepped impatiently out of his briefs. She didn't need glasses to read the signs of surging male hunger in him, and her own body responded to it. He sat down beside her on the edge of the bed and spread his fingers across her stomach. He seemed both possessive and at the same time entranced. Jamie shivered.

Cade reached out with his other hand, caught hers and brought her fingers to his thigh. Jamie needed no further encouragement. She stroked upward, delighting in the ripple of sensation that coursed through him at her touch. His skin was excitingly textured with dark, crisp hair. She could feel the long, smooth swell of muscle in his upper leg. When she dared to cup him intimately in the palm of her hand, he groaned heavily and stretched out beside her. His mouth found hers while he slowly grazed her nipple with the pad of his thumb. The sensual strength in his body was a driving force in the room.

"I've spent too many nights remembering how you react when I touch you," Cade gritted, and then his probing tongue was invading the territory behind her lips, reestablishing his right to complete intimacy.

Jamie moaned softly and her leg shifted, twining itself around his. Cade's hand slid down her breast, finding the already taut nipples and pausing to hold the fullness of her. Then his hand continued downward, following the path that led toward the dampening heat at the apex of her thighs. When his strong, sensitive fingers suddenly flicked across the exquisitely vulnerable focus of her erotic feelings, Jamie cried out and set her teeth lightly against his shoulder.

"Little vixen. Go ahead and use your teeth on me. You'll only succeed in setting me even more on fire." He nipped passionately at the curve of her throat, returning the sexy caress in full measure.

"Cade, I'm going out of my head. I thought I'd forgotten how it was between us."

"I won't let you forget again," he vowed. His fingers stroked deeply, intimately, until her whole body was lifting and arching in response. "That's it, sweetheart. I want to see you go up in flames. I've missed your heat so much."

Jamie's breath came more quickly, and her aroused body moved with unconscious invitation as she twisted in sensual torment. With growing abandon she pulled Cade's mouth back down to her own, her fingers locking in the thickness of his hair.

"Tell me how much you want me, honey," he ordered softly as his body strained against hers.

"Come to me Cade. I want you. More than I realized. More than I could possibly admit."

A part of her mind knew that if he had asked for words of love she would have been compelled to give them to him along with the words of need. But Cade didn't ask for them and the dangerous words remained unsaid.

"In the future you're going to learn just how easy it is to tell me you want me. By morning you will have had a lot of practice." Cade shifted, covering her body heavily with his own. "Wrap yourself around me, sweetheart. Give yourself to me."

He moved between her legs aggressively, making a place for himself between her soft, warm thighs, and then he paused as if savoring the moment. Jamie looked up at him through her passion-heavy lashes and saw the flaring gold in his eyes. Anticipation, satisfaction and desire were reflected in Cade's tawny gaze.

He was reclaiming what he felt he owned, Jamie realized suddenly. Before she could deny that claim by word or action, he was moving to stake it. She gasped as she felt the hardened power of his manhood thrust heavily into her softness.

"Cade!"

His mouth took hers again, swallowing her small cry. Jamie felt the surging rhythm he imposed on her and gave herself up to it. She loved him, and in this moment of ultimate intimacy she could not pretend otherwise. Jamie was unaware of the tiny marks she made in Cade's bronzed back as her passion took control. She only knew there was nothing else in the world to compare with having Cade Santerre make love to her. She gloried in his desire, his undisguised need of her, and she took infinite pleasure in her own flaring passion.

Heedlessly, recklessly, totally, she surrendered to the demands he was making on her. At the same time she generated her own demands, and he answered them hungrily, making it clear he wanted to please.

For a timeless interval they drank thirstily of each other, engaged in a sensual battle that brought the shared excitement to higher and higher levels.

Then the spiraling, tightening sensation deep in Jamie's body spun abruptly out of control, dragging her into the vortex of a throbbing, tumultuous storm. It was the same storm she had encountered that night on the yacht six weeks ago, and it brought the same sob of wonder to her lips. She sensed the man above her lose his fierce control.

With a muffled shout of satisfaction, Cade followed her into the heart of the whirling winds of passion. For an endless time they had the universe to themselves. And afterward Jamie refused to open her eyes. She nestled into the welcoming heat of Cade's arms and went to sleep. When all was said and done, this was the way it was supposed to be.

Awareness returned a long time later, when a shaft of light from the bathroom angled across the bed. Stirring sleepily, Jamie turned over and belatedly realized she was in her own bed. Memories of the night filtered back with disconcerting suddenness.

There had been the strange nightmare and then there had been Cade. Jamie shook her head, trying to clear the remnants of sleep from it. The bed was empty beside her.

"Cade?"

"In here," he called from the bathroom. "Just wanted a glass of water. I'll be right back."

She heard the door of the mirrored cabinet open, and then there was silence from the other room. Jamie blinked in the darkness and snuggled back down into the pillows. But now she was wide awake, her mind alive with the problem she had created for herself tonight.

She had just allowed herself to be drawn back into the arms of a man who had once callously used her; a man whose arrogance knew few bounds; a man she had promised herself she would not allow back into her life unless she was in full control of him. She had meant to keep sex out of the picture until she was convinced she could handle it.

It would be simpler to pretend to be asleep when he emerged from the bathroom. Jamie had a feeling it would be difficult enough to deal with Cade Santerre in the morning, let alone the middle of the night. When you weren't sure how to handle a volatile situation it was best to put it off for a while. Determinedly she kept her eyes closed.

But she wasn't going to have the opportunity of postponing the inevitable confrontation.

"What the hell is this?"

Cade's gritted question was laced with fury. A small object landed on the quilt a few inches from Jamie's wide-open eyes. At the same moment the overhead light blazed as Cade hit the switch.

Startled, Jamie levered herself up on one elbow. Her unfocused eyes went from Cade's thunderous features to the object he had tossed down on the bed. She couldn't see well enough without her glasses to read the printing on the box, but she knew by its general size and shape what it was.

"My birth control pills," she answered with a calm she was far from feeling.

"I can see that. How long have you been taking them?"

"Cade, what's the matter with you? Why are you so enraged?" She stared at him in confusion, trying to understand what was happening. This was the last reaction she had expected. Possessiveness, arrogance, satisfaction—any of a variety of masculine emotions would have seemed within the realm of probability from what she knew of Cade Santerre. But not this fury over a bottle of pills.

"How long have you been taking them?" he repeated savagely.

"I took them this summer," she said simply. No need to mention that she had gone off them last month on the assumption she wouldn't be needing them again for a long while.

"You were taking them this summer? You were on them when I made love to you that last night on the yacht?"

Jamie licked her lips, aware of the shimmering tension in him, but unable to comprehend the reason behind it. "Yes."

"That's impossible!"

"Why?" she asked blankly.

"Because you're supposed to be pregnant!" he roared.

FIVE

"Pregnant!" Jamie could only stare at him, stunned. "You thought I was pregnant?"

"It was the most logical explanation," Cade bit out roughly. He stalked across the room and flung himself into a chair. Totally unconcerned with his own nakedness he sprawled there, watching Jamie through brooding, narrowed eyes. "The timing was right."

"Timing?" she asked helplessly. Cade's state of undress might not bother him but her own similar condition was beginning to make her feel quite vulnerable. Jamie held the sheet to her breasts while she leaned over the edge of the bed and scrabbled around on the floor for the expensive French nightie.

"Six weeks," he explained impatiently. "It took you six weeks to come looking for me. That's about the length of time it would take you to suspect you might be pregnant."

"You're an authority on that sort of thing?"

"I had high-school biology just like everyone else!"

"I think you went to a more progressive high school than I did," she tried flippantly.

"This is not a joke, damn it!"

Jamie's hand closed around the gossamer material of the gown and she sat up quickly, tugging it over her head. "I don't understand, Cade. I told you I came to find you because Miss Isabel wanted you to verify her brother's suicide. Where did you get the idea I was pregnant?"

"I've just told you where I got the idea! Because of the amount of time that had elapsed," he nearly shouted. "And because I knew I had uncovered a streak of dumb, stubborn female pride in you. I figured that because of it, you would resist coming back to me as long as you could. When you showed up in six weeks, I decided it must be because you'd discovered you were pregnant. Otherwise, I'd decided, you'd probably wait two or three months. Long enough for your pride to have a chance to die down and for you to realize... Oh, forget it."

Slowly light began to dawn in Jamie's confused brain. She saw the beginnings of a way to salvage control and pride. She crouched on the bed, staring at him. "I see. You thought you had me all figured out, didn't you? Analyzed, pigeonholed and under control. Cade, the Great Manipulator. I don't know what makes you think you're such a good judge of other people's motives and actions! Whatever gave you the idea you understood me so well you could predict my behavior down to the minute?"

"I spent two months getting to know you, damn it!

Two whole months," he repeated bluntly. "At the end of which I had you in the palm of my hand. I know I did. Don't you dare deny it."

A wave of impotent anger washed over Jamie. He spoke the truth and they both knew it. She would have done anything for him at the end of those two months. Desperately she struggled for a loophole. "If you knew me so well, why didn't you guess I was taking birth-control pills?"

"The subject never arose," he muttered.

"So you just assumed I'd plunge into a passionate little interlude with you without bothering to protect myself? Cade, I'm twenty-nine years old and I'm not exactly stupid, despite some recent evidence to the contrary. I knew within a few days of meeting you that the odds were good I'd wind up in bed with you. I went to a doctor and got a prescription."

"Why didn't you say anything about it?" he demanded.

"It's not exactly the sort of thing one casually mentions over the dinner table. Not to a man who hasn't yet asked you to go to bed with him," Jamie said between clenched teeth. She concentrated on the cloisonné jar beside him, unwilling to meet his eyes. "Actually, you never did ask. You just sort of assumed I'd follow where you led." *Right into bed,* she added silently.

"I get it. It didn't strike you as terribly romantic, right?" he mocked, concentrating on her first complaint and ignoring the second. "'I had a wonderful evening, Cade. By the way, I'm taking the pill, just in case you're interested in hopping into bed'"

"You see what I mean?" Jamie responded austerely. "It has a tacky sound to it. Getting accidentally pregnant is even tackier, however. Tacky is not romantic." She'd had two months to anticipate that one night with Cade. Two months of knowing where the relationship with him would lead. Two months of knowing she was falling in love and realizing where that love was bound to lead.

Cade swore softly. "I can't believe I didn't realize you'd been busy behind the scenes making plans and taking precautions."

"That's because you seem to have formed the impression that I'm some kind of naive, romantic, empty-headed little bit of fluff. I'm a woman, Cade. I can think for myself. And I can take care of myself." Proudly she swung her gaze back to meet his, but without her glasses the effect was somewhat diminished. All she could really detect in his face was the brooding storm that seemed to be simmering there.

"So you're not pregnant?" he pressed once more.

She shook her head, wondering at the strange combination of frustration and dashed hope in his voice. This was not quite what a woman expected when she assured a man she wasn't pregnant. Men were reputed to be exceedingly relieved in such circumstances. "I should think you'd be grateful."

He ignored that. "You really came looking for me just to offer me this crazy job of Miss Isabel's?" He sounded dazed now.

"That's the only reason," Jamie emphasized.

"Then why did you come traipsing across the hall tonight?" he demanded. "Straight into my arms and my bed?"

Feeling braver and more sure of herself by the second as she witnessed the corresponding uncertainty in Cade, Jamie seized the opportunity. "I had a bad dream. I decided to get a glass of milk or something from the kitchen. Almost as soon as I stepped out of my bedroom, you appeared."

"And you figured, what the hell, why not jump into bed with me again since I'm conveniently located, obviously willing and you're on the pill?"

Jamie sucked in her breath and stuck to her newly developing image. There seemed to be a measure of safety in it. "Any objections?" Uneasily her fingers curled around the small box lying beside her. Belatedly she began to wonder how long the effects of the contraceptive lasted after a woman stopped taking pills. Especially when she'd only been on them a short time. Mentally she counted the days since she had gone off the medication. It had definitely been almost a month now.

"I can hardly object, can I? I got what I wanted."

"Did you?" Jamie edged her feet out from under the covers and sat up on the side of the bed. "Will you be leaving in the morning, then?"

His eyes narrowed dangerously. "I'll think about it."

"You do that!" Now she was getting angry.

"Jamie, don't push me."

She flicked him a curious glance. "You're really furious, aren't you?"

"Why should I be furious?"

"Come on, Cade. You look like you'd enjoy chewing on nails." Jamie's sense of insight deepened. "There is no logical reason why you should be angry except for one thing."

"What's that?" he challenged coolly.

"You may have gotten what you wanted but you didn't get it for the reasons you assumed you were getting it."

"You're not making any sense," he told her repressively.

Jamie nodded her head once in growing comprehension. "It's throwing you, isn't it?"

"What's throwing me?"

"The knowledge that I didn't come looking for you because I was pregnant, or because I couldn't bring myself to give up our relationship. I came looking for you for purely business reasons, and you don't like that one little bit. It means you missed something this summer when you were busy analyzing, assessing and seducing me. You failed to properly pigeonhole me and therefore you failed to predict my actions properly. That makes you nervous because you pride yourself on being able to manipulate and control people. You can't manipulate and control someone whose motives you can't fully analyze, can you, Cade? You got me back into bed but you're not quite sure why I'm there, and that makes you fretful, doesn't it? Well, you don't have to worry the problem to death. I'll be glad to explain."

"I can't wait."

"It's simple enough," she declared loftily. "Physical attraction. You don't have to look any further than that for a logical explanation. I'm not pregnant and I didn't find myself unable to live without you. I do, however, find you still physically attractive. As long as you're living in such convenient proximity as you are tonight, I suppose it's not unreasonable to expect me to traipse across the hall now and again." In that moment it seemed a near-brilliant excuse for her actions this evening. Why hadn't she thought of it before? Physical attraction. No need to admit to love.

She didn't need glasses to see the dark red color that stained his face. A little late, Jamie's new perception warned her that she might have gone too far with that last taunting remark. But she had been unable to hold her tongue. She'd found a way to recoup some of her crumbling emotional defenses and she'd grabbed it with both hands, making it sound as though she saw nothing wrong in treating Cade Santerre as a casual and occasional lover.

"You're saying that's all this was tonight? A mildly entertaining one-night stand?" he asked dangerously.

"Why should it mean any more to me than it did to you?" She shrugged. "That's all our affair was for you this summer, wasn't it? A convenient one-night stand?"

Cade came out of the chair and was across the room in three long strides. He reached her before she could get to her feet. Seizing her by the shoulders, he hauled her up to stand in front of him. "I spent two full months working toward that one night. I planned that night right down to the fifty dollar bottle of cognac I had on hand in the galley for an after-dinner drink. I had to slip the maître d' at the restaurant ten bucks just to get the seat you liked by the window. I had to order those yellow roses I gave you before dinner a week ahead of time at the florist's. You were like melted butter in my hands this summer. It was no casual roll in the hay for you and you know it."

Jamie held on to her pride and her temper. A strange, driving force was motivating her now. She had no trouble putting a name to it. Revenge. Jamie was learning that when a woman found herself cornered it was possible to want a little revenge even though she was passionately in love.

"I had no idea you spent so much money in one evening! Trust an accountant to have it all tabulated right down to the penny."

His fingers flexed on her shoulders. "At the time I thought it was worth every penny."

"Summer was a long time ago," she said.

"Six weeks isn't very long."

"Believe it or not, six weeks is quite long enough to get over a man who used me the way you did. Actually six hours took care of most of the problem. By the end of six days I was totally cured. I came looking for you yesterday for one reason and one reason only. Miss Isabel assigned me the job."

"And you always do what Miss Isabel tells you to do?" he growled.

"As long as I work for her, yes." Jamie tried to sound cool about it. "In this case, it wasn't all that traumatic having to carry out her instructions. In spite of what you seemed to have assumed, I suffered no lingering effects from that night on the yacht, either emotional or physical."

"But when you saw me again you did manage to recall that the sex was pretty good, is that it?"

"That's it," she agreed blandly.

"And tonight you just decided to let yourself enjoy it again? No strings attached this time?"

"Why not?"

"I don't believe you." Cade's words were laced with steel and ice.

"You can, of course, believe anything you wish. I know how pleasant self-deception can be. I certainly had enough experience with it this summer. I'll give you some advice, however. It's risky to paint things in a falsely romantic light. Very naive, Cade. Leads to all sorts of rude awakenings. You taught me that. If I were you, I'd pay attention to your own excellent lessons on the subject."

"I'm not the one who's prone to view the world through romantic lenses, damn it!"

"I don't have that problem any longer myself," she assured him easily.

"You expect me to believe that in six weeks you've transformed yourself into a cool, tough little lady who can handle a casual affair on her own terms?"

"Safer than letting you handle that kind of affair on your terms, isn't it? Safer for me, that is. If you decide you don't mind the fact that you're no longer in control of my emotions and able to manipulate me at will, then stick around, Cade. Who knows? This time we might manage a rational, even-handed affair that won't leave either one of us feeling the fool when it's over. If that sort of straightforward, honest arrangement doesn't appeal to you, then you'd better leave."

His mouth hardened. "Because if I stay you'll run the show?"

"I won't play the role of melted butter again," she vowed. "You'll never hold me in the palm of your hand a second time, Cade Santerre. I'm not quite as naive and empty-headed as you seemed to have assumed."

Without waiting for his response, Jamie swung around on one heel and walked out of the bedroom. Her head tilted proudly, her pulse racing with adrenaline, her stomach twisting with tension, she headed straight back across the hall, opened the door to Miss Isabel's room and shut it decisively behind her.

Then she collapsed into a trembling heap on the bed. It had been a grand exit but it had taken nearly everything she'd had to pull it off successfully.

Pride, revenge and the need to assert some control over the man who had once hurt her so badly had kept her going during the confrontation. But alone in the bedroom it was difficult to keep the fires of pride and revenge burning at their hottest. Sitting forlornly on the edge of the bed, Jamie was aware of a chill that seemed to seep all the way into her bones.

Cade had assumed she was pregnant. He thought that, knowing she was going to have his baby, she had lowered her defenses far enough to dream up an excuse to get in touch with him again. And if that hadn't worked, he would just as confidently have expected her to show up in a few more weeks, simply because she couldn't bear to end the affair.

He must think she was truly a mindless little twit at the mercy of her feminine emotions, Jamie told herself violently.

If he could see her now, he'd know he wasn't far off in that assessment. She was shivering with reaction and cold. What would he do now, she wondered unhappily. She'd as good as told him that if he stayed it would be on her terms, and that her terms involved treating their relationship as a very casual sexual affair. Nothing more.

Cade wouldn't like that. It wasn't that he had any qualms about treating her callously or casually, she reminded herself. But he'd savagely resent being treated that way himself. He was far too accustomed to being the one working the strings.

At every point this past summer he had set the pace, manipulating her emotions with consummate ease until she was practically begging for him on every level. Melted butter. Jamie winced, recalling how wrapped up in him she had been. She would have done anything for him. She had fallen in love with the man. Never in her life had she been so much involved with another human being. Never had she wanted to give herself so completely. At the time it had seemed totally rational.

With a sigh Jamie reached out to switch on the bedside light. She'd better find her glasses before she accidentally stepped on them. Frowning, she peered down at the white carpet beside the bed. She must have brushed them off the night table at some point.

Unable to spot the chic frames, she got down on her hands and knees and began to grope around under the bed. Her fingers closed over the glasses just as the bedroom door opened behind her.

"Jamie?" Cade's inquiry was gruff. There was a pause as he looked around the room for her. Then he spotted her. "What are you doing?"

"Looking for my glasses. I couldn't find them earlier this evening when I had that nightmare." She pushed the frames onto her nose and got to her feet, aware of the see-through quality of the nightgown. Trying to appear unselfconscious, she walked quickly across the room to yank a robe out of Miss Isabel's closet. Hastily she donned the garment. Cade, she was relieved to see, had pulled on a pair of jeans.

"I came to talk to you about that nightmare you said you had," Cade began a little too casually.

Jamie's head snapped up as she finished tying the sash of the robe. The bland expression on his face didn't fool her for a moment. "Still looking for angles? I didn't make up that bit about having had a bad dream and I definitely did not use it as an excuse to throw myself into your arms, if that's what you're thinking."

"I just wanted to ask you about it," he said, but she could tell she'd effectively cut off his latest tactic. He'd obviously been about to convince himself that she'd run instinctively into his arms when she'd been afraid. No telling what he might do with such an assumption. That was Cade to the core. Always looking for a motive so that he could manipulate.

"Forget the nightmare. I've got an interesting question to ask you," Jamie said before he could pursue his own line of logic. "What on earth would you have done if I'd shown up pregnant at the marina?" She hadn't actually meant to ask that question. Jamie wasn't certain she wanted to hear the answer. She'd probably get some assurance that he would gladly have footed the bill for an abortion.

He gave her a long, steady look. "Married you."

"Married me!" Thoroughly astounded at the answer, Jamie found herself staring openmouthedly at him.

"What else?" he growled. Then he moved, stepping past her toward the French door that opened onto the terrace. "It's freezing in here. For pete's sake. Why is the door open? Are you trying to make yourself sick?"

Still struggling to assimilate what he had just said, Jamie turned to watch him. Belatedly she realized that one of the glass-paned doors was indeed standing ajar. That fact finally registered just as Cade slammed and locked the door. Jamie swallowed, her mouth abruptly quite dry.

"Cade, I didn't open that door."

He glanced at her over his shoulder, frowning. "What do you mean, you didn't open it?"

"Just what I said." Weakly Jamie sank down into a white, curving chair. "About that nightmare, Cade. Maybe...maybe we should talk about it."

"It has something to do with the door being open?" he demanded, moving back across the oddly shaped room to drop into the chair opposite hers.

Jamie chewed reflectively on her lower lip and glanced uneasily up at the portrait that occupied the wall between the two white chairs. "I know this sounds crazy but when I woke up..." She broke off and tried again, because obviously she couldn't have been fully awake when she'd seen the portrait come alive. "I mean, just before I really woke up the thing that made me nervous was the funny sensation that Hadley's picture here sort of, well, moved."

"Moved?" Cade watched her warily. "What do you mean, moved? The whole picture shifted position?"

Jamie shook her head. "Not quite," she said, feeling embarrassed, which only angered her further. She was very conscious of needing to maintain a cool reserved image in front of Cade. Anything less and he would pounce. This sort of thing could become very stressful, she realized. "It was more an impression that the man in the portrait moved. For a while after I first woke up, I thought there might be two portraits. That was probably the effects of double vision, though," she explained hastily. "Sometimes that happens when I'm not wearing my glasses. I have to concentrate to focus properly, especially in darkness. It was just one of those things, Cade. A bad dream. To be honest, it bothered me enough that I wanted to get out of the room for a few minutes."

"Which is how you wound up standing in the hall outside my door at two in the morning, wearing something that looks like it came from Fredericks of Hollywood?"

"This gown was designed in Paris!" Incensed, Jamie momentarily forgot the nightmare of Hadley's portrait. "Paris, *France*, you heathen! And it cost a fortune! I did not get it out of some Fredericks of Hollywood catalog. I spent days shopping for it at the most exclusive boutiques in Santa Barbara!"

"Santa Barbara? You bought it this past summer?" The tawny eyes were suddenly quite brilliantly gold.

"At about the same time I got the prescription for those damn pills," Jamie confirmed bitterly. Then she realized it would also have been around the same time he had been buying a fifty-dollar bottle of cognac and ordering perfect yellow roses. Talk about irony. They'd each privately spent small fortunes preparing for that evening.

"You're saying you bought the nightgown to wear for me?" Cade asked gently.

"I got my money's worth out of the pills but I didn't out of the nightgown," she informed him in what she hoped was a suitably sarcastic tone of voice. "You may recall we went directly back to the *Dreamer II* after we left the restaurant. I couldn't figure out a way to pack the gown without seeming a tad obvious. I've been wearing it a lot lately so I wouldn't feel that I wasted the two hundred ninety-seven dollars and ninety-eight cents."

Cade looked dumbfounded. "Two hundred and ninety-seven dollars? For a nightie?"

"And ninety-eight cents. Say no more, Cade. I fully agree with what you're thinking. An utter waste of money. I tried to take it back the day after you left town, but the shop wouldn't refund my money," she explained flippantly. That was an outright fabrication. She'd had her hands full, dealing with her hurt and anger as well as trying to comfort Miss Isabel and fight off reporters. She had forgotten all about the nightgown until she'd discovered it in her suitcase when she'd unpacked here at the house.

"Two hundred and ninety-seven dollars for a nightie," Cade repeated, still sounding dazed. "To wear for me."

"As you have noted more than once, I was a romantic little idiot this summer. Could we please get back to the subject at hand? It's nearly five o'clock in the morning."

Slowly but obediently Cade nodded. "The door."

"Yes. The door. I didn't open it, Cade." She was very sure of that. The knowledge sent a chill down her spine.

"Any chance it had been left open earlier? After all, you just got back to the house yourself a few hours ahead of me. Had you been in this room before you moved in for the night?"

"No, I hadn't wandered in here," Jamie admitted,

dark brows making an intent line above the rims of her glasses. "I suppose it's possible Annie opened it and forgot to lock it the last time she was here."

"Annie?"

"Annie is the woman who comes in to clean once a week."

"She probably wouldn't remember one way or the other," Cade muttered.

"No. She might have left it open. But I didn't notice it earlier when I was getting ready for bed," Jamie said, trying to think. "Of course, if it was only un-latched, not actually standing open, I might not have been aware of it. A gust of wind could have blown it ajar later."

"About the same time you thought you were seeing Hadley's portrait move?" Cade asked quietly.

She gave him a quick, hopeful look. "You think the wind might have made the portrait shift, too?"

Cade idly reached out to push experimentally against the heavy frame of the big painting. It didn't budge. "No," he stated categorically. "I don't think a small gust of wind would have made this sucker move."

"I didn't think so." Jamie's mouth curved wryly. "Miss Isabel and I had a heck of a time getting it hung in the first place. Weighs a ton."

"When did Miss Isabel do it?" Cade examined the strange conglomeration of objects embedded in the acrylic paint. "The date on that letter is fairly recent."

"She did it when we got back from Santa Barbara. Worked night and day, poor thing. I think she was trying to deal with her grief. It was after she finished it that she started talking about the possibility of Hadley still being alive. He was the only family she had, and I guess she couldn't bring herself to believe he'd gone. I could tell she needed to have it confirmed so that she would be able to accept the facts and get on with her own life." Jamie stopped talking, aware that she was perilously close to saying too much on that score. The last thing she wanted to surface just now was the exact manner in which the idea of hiring Cade Santerre had been put into Miss Isabel's brain.

"So when she came up with the bright idea of having me investigate, you let her talk you into it," Cade concluded in a flat tone of voice.

"Uh, yes. Something like that." Determinedly Jamie pressed on to the next subject that had occurred to her. "There's one other thing, Cade. I didn't think too much of it at the time, but now I'm not so sure."

He gave her a patiently inquiring glance. "Go on."

"Well, yesterday when I stopped for groceries outside of San Simeon, I caught a fleeting glimpse of someone at the gas pump who reminded me a little of Hadley."

Cade jumped on that, the hard planes of his face tightening abruptly. "He only reminded you a little of Fitzgerald?"

"I just got a small glimpse and I only saw the back of his head. But his hair was the same color and the general build of the man was similar. There was something about the way he carried himself that actually put me in mind of Hadley." When Cade said nothing, merely continued to watch her, Jamie shook her head in self-denial. "No, it couldn't have been him. It was just my imagination. Besides, even if he were alive, why would he show up around here?"

"Looking for his sister."

"But he knows I'd be with her. If he wanted to keep everyone thinking the suicide was for real, he wouldn't dare let me see him."

"He undoubtedly knows of your beyond-the-call-of-duty sense of loyalty to Miss Isabel," Cade observed dryly. "He might figure he could count on that if you should become aware of him."

"That really bothers you, doesn't it?" Jamie muttered.

"Your sense of loyalty to your employer? I've told you I think it's a little extreme. Not to mention misplaced. But it fits in with your general view of life, I suppose. You'd have done well in the age of chivalry and honor when unquestioning loyalty was a virtue."

"Perhaps," she shot back caustically. "But I'm finally learning to adjust to my own era. You've already taught me not to believe in knights in shining armor, for example."

Cade closed his eyes for a prolonged instant, and Jamie honestly couldn't tell if he was concealing genuine pain or blazing fury. When he lifted his lashes, the tawny gaze was unreadable, but the force with which his powerful hands gripped the arms of the chair was evident in the paleness around the knuckles.

"Are you going to slash me with that sharp little

tongue of yours every chance you get?" he asked with almost detached interest.

"Possibly," Jamie retorted. "No, *probably*. It's the new me."

"A harsh mistress," he murmured.

Jamie lifted her head angrily. "I'm not your mistress."

He shrugged. "Lover?"

"At the moment," she snapped, "I am the woman who is supervising your work for my employer. I suggest you start performing in an investigative capacity or head south to your boat."

He got to his feet with a lithe movement, his features set in cold, austere lines. "Yes, ma'am. Since it's almost dawn, I think I'll take a shower and get dressed. I will go to work as soon as a few offices in Los Angeles are open. I'll try to do a reasonably satisfactory job for you, Jamie."

He was at the door of her bedroom before Jamie could find the last words. "Just do as good a job proving Hadley's dead as you did ruining him in the first place, and I'll be satisfied."

Cade, who had fully intended to shut the door behind him quite coolly, wound up slamming it instead. Furiously he stormed across the hall and then slammed the door of the room he had been using. Shocked at the lack of control, he came to a halt in the middle of Jamie's bedroom and stared down at his hands. His fingers were almost trembling with the force of his anger and frustration.

"Settle down and think, Santerre," he chided himself. "Losing your self-control isn't going to do any good. Damn it to hell. What a mess."

He stripped off his jeans and headed for the shower. First things first. He needed to calm down and start dealing rationally with the situation, or else he would be farther up the creek without a paddle than he already was.

He found the burgundy-and-white tiled bathroom pleasantly littered with Jamie's personal choices in soap, shampoo, hair rinse and body lotions. They were all exotically scented and flamboyantly packaged by shrewd manufacturers who knew how to appeal to the romantic element in a woman's nature. The names on the bottles conjured up mysterious locales, seductive sensations and heady fragrances. Cade was momentarily fascinated with the assortment. He was seeing a private side of Jamie that he'd never before had a chance to investigate. Although, he thought in satisfaction, if anyone had invited him to describe her bathroom sight unseen, he would have come fairly close to the reality. He'd have guessed it would look something like this.

He sniffed a soap that was carved in the shape of a rose. Sure enough, it smelled like a rose. He dropped it back in the seashell dish and picked up Jamie's hair rinse. It reminded him of peaches. Methodically he went through the array of lotions and potions, opening jars and inhaling the scents. The woman must have spent a month's salary on this stuff, Cade decided. That thought reminded him of the concoction of lace and satin she had worn to bed.

Two hundred and ninety-seven dollars for a nightie! And she'd bought it this past summer to wear for him. Too bad he hadn't given her a chance to pick it up and bring it with her the night he'd taken her back to the yacht and made love to her!

Cade set down the last of the bottles, opting to use the lemon-scented soap on the grounds that it would be the least objectionable scent on a man.

She must have purchased that nightie while under the influence of a particularly reckless state of romantic anticipation, Cade thought as he soaped himself. He wrinkled his nose in mild disgust as the lemon scent permeated the shower.

It would be like Jamie to do that sort of thing. If she had made up her mind to cast herself wholeheartedly into the fires of a passionate affair, she would exert every effort to make everything perfect.

Cade paused, staring unseeingly at the line of burgundy tile in front of him. Water cascaded down his chest as he considered his last thought. That explained the birth-control pills, of course. After all, she'd seen that night on board the yacht coming for two months. He'd made no secret of his desire. It had been only a matter of time, and they'd both known it. Jamie, being a woman, would have had to consider possible consequences. She probably hadn't wanted to spoil the romantic illusion by discussing such a mundane matter with him. Hadn't she admitted a few minutes ago that she'd found it a difficult topic to bring up in casual conversation when the man involved hadn't yet issued the invitation to bed? The problem was that he simply hadn't viewed the situation from this perspective. That explained why he'd been laboring under a false assumption.

Absently Cade began to shave himself, going by instinct as his mind worked on the problem. A woman's whole nature didn't alter in the course of six weeks, he assured himself. Jamie's gentle, romantic nature was too fundamental to change in that short a time. Just look at all this junk in her bathroom.

And remember the way she had unfolded like a flower in his arms last night. A passionflower. Once back in his bed, she had been the same Jamie he had been seeing in his dreams for six long weeks. During the night she had held him with hot desire and shimmering need. She had given herself to him completely, just as she had that night on the yacht. His body started to react just at the memory. With a grimace he turned off the hot-water tap and let the shower go cold. After a couple of moments of the drastic treatment Cade reached out to turn off the water and shook the spray out of his hair. He groped for a towel and came up with a fluffy burgundy one that had a rose embroidered on it. Briskly he went to work with it, trying to marshal his thoughts.

All right, he decided grimly, so he'd underestimated the full extent of her anger. He should have realized that her passion for revenge and her fear of getting hurt again would be strong. After all, she was a woman in every sense of the word. Passionate, intelligent, proud and not a little reckless in some ways. None of that contradicted his assessment of her basic

nature. He just hadn't made proper allowance for the
full strength of that nature.

Cade slung the towel over the rack and glanced in
the mirror to make certain the shaving job had been
accurate. Satisfied, he walked back out into the bedroom and began to dress.

The only real miscalculation he'd made so far was in
assuming she was pregnant, he told himself as he
tugged on a dark-hued pullover. Stupid of him, really.
What were the odds that a woman would get pregnant
after spending one night with a man, even if she
hadn't been using a contraceptive? Probably exceedingly slim. He glowered at himself in the mirror.
Dumb assumption. Dumb high-school biology class.
The teacher probably had just been trying to terrorize
the students when she'd warned them all those years
ago about how easy it was for a woman to get pregnant.

Cade sighed, wondering briefly how he'd managed
to convince himself so completely that he'd gotten Jamie pregnant. He wasn't usually naive, nor did he normally jump to conclusions without evidence. He
promptly dismissed that useless line of inquiry.

It led, however, to another issue. His glowering expression intensified as he zipped up his jeans and fastened the snap. Jamie had seemed quite startled at the
notion of him offering marriage in the event she was
pregnant.

That bothered him, Cade realized. What the hell did
she think he would do? Toss her out into the cold? If
he hadn't wanted her to get pregnant, he would have

taken preventive measures himself. She should have understood that. She should have trusted him to take care of her. She must not have much faith in his willingness to carry out his responsibilities.

Somehow that last realization irritated him more than anything else. Damn it, she ought to have known that he would have taken care of her.

Perhaps not, he thought savagely. She hadn't believed that he'd never intended for her to get caught in the crunch when the authorities moved in on Hadley. Given that, it made sense that she might not believe he would really have offered marriage if he'd gotten her pregnant. The little idiot.

Swearing in exasperation, Cade swung around to head out of the room in search of breakfast. Okay, so he'd made a false assumption and a tactical miscalculation or two. That didn't change the basic situation.

He'd spent two months this past summer seducing Jamie Garland. He was a patient man. He'd do it all over again, if necessary. But this time around he wouldn't deny himself the warmth of her bed for long. A man had his limits.

SIX

Jamie realized with disgust that she was having to devote an unnatural amount of concentration to the simple routine of getting breakfast ready. She found herself intently gnawing on her lower lip while watching the toast browning under the oven broiler and tried to shake off the sensation that things were on the verge of getting out of control. She was only fixing breakfast, for heaven's sake, not working on a solution to the problem of the national debt.

But everything seemed to be requiring undue caution this morning. It was as if she dare not relax or something would blow up in her face. Maybe this was what people meant when they said they felt as though they were walking on eggs. Even the simple act of showering and pulling on a pair of jeans and an oversize blue work shirt had taken more than the necessary amount of attention. Her hair still wasn't right. After several attempts in front of the mirror Jamie had abandoned her efforts, and now the dark auburn mass was clamped in an exceedingly casual twist. Tendrils were already coming loose.

It was all Cade's fault. He had been a disturbing influence in her life since the moment she had met him. Matters were not improving with time. They would disintegrate entirely if he ever discovered that it had been her idea, not Miss Isabel's, to contact him with the offer of a job.

Jamie yanked the rack partway out from under the broiler, flipped the toast and shoved it back. She wondered if Cade liked peanut-butter toast for breakfast.

On the other hand, she asked herself resolutely, who cared what he liked for breakfast? He could take it or leave it. That was supposed to be part of the new arrangement. Casual. Sophisticated. Independent. The second time around with Cade was going to be on her terms. She might not be able to resist playing with fire but she would darn well run the risks in her own way, not his. Last time he had played the tune and she had danced to his measure. This time the process was going to be reversed.

Jamie pushed her glasses more firmly onto her nose as she straightened away from the oven, and then she went to the refrigerator to find the carton of freshly ground peanut butter. The whole problem, she realized forlornly, was that it was almost impossible to be casual, sophisticated and completely independent around Cade. Take now, for instance. A part of her did care about fixing him a breakfast he would enjoy.

It made no sense at all. The man deserved absolutely no consideration from her. But telling herself that indisputable truth did not absolve her of the uneasy feeling that she had been unfair to him early this morning. That crack about telling him to do as good a job of proving Hadley Fitzgerald dead as he had done ruining the man in first place had been rather harsh. When all was said and done, it wasn't exactly Cade's fault that Hadley had apparently been a very shady businessman.

If only Hadley had not been Miss Isabel's brother and if only Miss Isabel wasn't both her close friend and her employer, Jamie thought wistfully. And if only Cade hadn't spent two months seducing her while he was investigating Hadley. Life could be full of "if onlys."

"Something's burning."

Startled, Jamie jerked around as Cade spoke from the doorway. Simultaneously her nose caught the whiff of overdone bread. "Oh, Lord, the toast!" She darted over to the oven and pulled the rack out. The toast had been caught in time. Barely. It was definitely very dark but still edible.

"You should use a toaster. Then you wouldn't have to watch it so closely. You also wouldn't waste excess electricity by heating up the whole oven just to brown toast." Cade sauntered over to the counter and took one of the stools. He reached for the pot of coffee Jamie had just finished making.

"As usual, your advice is extremely well-timed, well thought out and highly intelligent," Jamie muttered. "However, I didn't ask for it."

He sipped coffee and watched her over the rim of

the cup. "Are you ever going to ask for anything from me, Jamie?"

"Not if I can help it. Do you like peanut-butter toast?" She began slathering peanut butter on a slice of darkly browned bread.

"For breakfast?"

"This isn't dinner I'm working on here."

He winced. "I love peanut-butter toast for breakfast."

"Then this is your lucky day."

"Jamie, honey, are you going to spend the whole day snapping at me?" Cade asked plaintively.

She looked up, glowering at him from behind her glasses. "I don't know. I suppose it will depend on how you behave yourself. Keep in mind that you're here to do a job, and perhaps we can make it through the day without slitting each other's throats."

"You're really determined to make sure I know who's boss this time around, aren't you?" he asked wonderingly.

"It seems the best way to prevent any unpleasant surprises such as I had to endure six weeks ago." Briskly she finished spreading peanut butter.

"Are you ever going to believe that I never meant things to end the way they did six weeks ago?"

"Oh, I believe that your pal Gallagher and his men apparently moved a little earlier than you had planned. I even believe it's possible you thought you'd have me out of the way the day the roof fell in on Hadley. But that doesn't change the fact that you used me. It also doesn't change the fact that you never told me the truth about why you were spending so much time with the Fitzgeralds. Our relationship lacked an essential element, Cade. It's called mutual trust."

"I did not use you. And as for telling you the truth about why I was hanging around Fitzgerald, I couldn't risk it. You would have felt it your duty to warn Isabel that her brother was in danger. I couldn't take a chance on your divided loyalties. The whole mess didn't concern you, anyway," Cade said bluntly.

"Didn't concern me! How can you say that? I was practically a member of the household," Jamie flared. "I was the one who had to fend off the reporters after you left. I was the one who had to help Miss Isabel cope with the fact that her brother had probably committed suicide. I was the one who had to deal with Mr. Gallagher and his men while they went through Hadley's private belongings. I was the one who had to close up the house in Santa Barbara. Shall I continue with the list of all the ways in which I was not involved in that mess?"

"I think we had better go back to discussing peanut butter on toast," Cade said with a sigh. "And then we can go on to discussing the job at hand."

Jamie flinched from the grimness in his voice. She wished she hadn't brought up the past, but unless she kept that firmly in mind she was in danger of forgetting it the way she had last night when he'd taken her in his arms. Last night should be a lesson to her. She had forgotten everything but the wonder of being in his arms again. Things were happening too fast this time around. Determinedly she faced him, the plate of peanut-butter toast in her hand.

"Cade, we need to make certain we understand each other. If you're going to finish this job for Miss Isabel..."

"I am."

"And if you're going to stay here while you do it..."

"I am."

"Then you must understand that the only way I can allow that is..."

"On your terms," he finished succinctly. He gave her a brooding, level glance. "I understand. I know you need to work it out."

She frowned. "Work what out?"

"The revenge. You have to have a chance to reassert yourself. I left you feeling used and vulnerable six weeks ago. God knows I didn't mean for you to feel that way, Jamie. I meant to keep you safe, clear of what was coming down. It didn't work out that way, and now you're wary and angry. I didn't think your resentment would go so deep or last this long. I guess I misjudged the situation between us, took too much for granted. I thought you would figure out for yourself that I really hadn't used you. I was wrong."

"You sound as though you're busy analyzing and assessing again," she grumbled, slicing toast. It made her uneasy to hear him admit that he might have been wrong. But it made her even more uneasy to hear him going through a logical reassessment of what it was he had done wrong.

"Analyzing and assessing situations is something I

usually do fairly well," Cade reminded her gently. "Apparently I blew it this time."

"A slight miscalculation. The same kind of mistake you made assuming I must be coming back to you because I was pregnant." She tossed the plate of toast onto the counter and stood on the opposite side, nibbling at her own breakfast.

Cade examined the peanut-butter toast. "As you said, a slight miscalculation. It doesn't change things, honey. The only thing it affects is timing."

"Timing?"

He looked up. "I need to give you time to work out your feelings. I'm willing to do that."

She shook her head wryly. "Even when you're *trying* to be humble, you can't quite manage it, can you?"

"Give me a chance, Jamie." There was a genuine plea in his quiet words. "That's all I'm asking. You're usually so willing to give everyone else in the world, including a crook like Fitzgerald, the benefit of a doubt. Why can't you extend the courtesy to me?"

Jamie hesitated. Across the counter their eyes met. She felt as though she were hovering on the edge of a precipice. The important thing to remember was, she decided, that she didn't have to choose between hurling herself over the edge or retreating completely. She could find another, safer way down the mountain. As long as she kept control of the situation and her own emotions, she would be able to make her own way off the edge. She had known from the beginning that approaching Cade Santerre a second time had to be done with great caution.

"We have to do it my way, Cade. And I'm making no guarantees."

Something cold and relentless flashed for an instant in the tawny gaze and then it was gone. "We'll do it your way, Jamie."

She munched toast for a moment before finding a way to break the unnatural silence that followed his comment. She wanted to ask for clarification, wanted to demand that he repeat what he'd just promised, but she was a little afraid to push it. "I suppose we should get down to business."

"I told you I'd call some people in L.A. after eight o'clock."

"That Gallagher person?" she hazarded.

"Yeah, Gallagher. He can update me. Maybe he's learned something useful in the past six weeks. After I left Santa Barbara I washed my hands of the whole mess. I also should make a start on whatever information I can dig up around here. I've been thinking about that business of your door being ajar."

"So have I," Jamie admitted, "and the more I think about it, the more certain I am that Annie must have unlocked it and forgotten to relock it before she left. It wouldn't be the first time she's made a simple mistake like that."

"What about your nightmare?"

"I've had lots of instances of double vision before, when I wasn't wearing my glasses," she said, shrugging. "I told you, I have trouble focusing properly without them." In the light of day it was easy to face that kind of logic.

"Well, maybe..."

"You said you wanted personal information on Hadley," Jamie went on, grateful for the change of topic.

"Does Miss Isabel keep photo albums or letters? Did she ever let her brother handle any of her own investments?"

"Sometimes," Jamie said slowly, answering the last question first.

"As the person who managed Miss Isabel's business affairs, were you ever approached by Hadley?"

"Everything Hadley recommended for his sister in the investment line was conservative and rock solid. She never suffered any significant losses because of his advice, and at various times she made a great deal of money. I never had enough spare cash to take any risks. My money's all in the bank. Hadley certainly never tried to take advantage of me. He used to say I was wise to bank my savings until I had enough to play with," Jamie defended stoutly.

Cade backed off, clearly reluctant to push her on that score. He was obviously going to resist the temptation to comment on her naïveté regarding Hadley. His hesitation to do so gave her courage. It was obvious she wasn't the only one trying to walk on eggs this morning. A part of her wondered at Cade's attempt at diplomacy. He was trying, Jamie realized with a start. He was making an effort to mend his side of the fence. The thought sent a rush of hope and longing through her that she couldn't banish completely, not even with a litany of repeated warnings.

"Okay, presumably he was fond of his sister and would not have involved her in any of his schemes. In his own right, Hadley was quite shrewd. There's no reason he wouldn't have given Miss Isabel sound advice. What I'm interested in are the records of the various transactions he might have recommended. I'd like to see which brokerage houses he told her to use, for example. What contacts he had. I'd like a look at the files of any of the real estate or investment deals he fixed up for her. I want the names of the people he used to conclude the arrangements. Were those records your responsibility?"

"Yes." Jamie concentrated on pouring herself a cup of coffee. "I can get those for you. Anything else?"

Cade considered his words. "Jamie, I'm not sure how to ask this without making you bristle..."

"Try." She discovered she liked it when he was being careful around her.

"Well, was there anything that Miss Isabel brought home from the house in Santa Barbara besides the baggage she arrived with at the beginning of the summer? Anything that might have belonged to Hadley?"

Jamie regarded him silently for a long moment. "Not exactly," she finally said.

Cade closed his eyes in what was obviously a silent plea for patience. "Not exactly. Care to expand on that a bit further?"

Jamie tapped one fingernail on the counter while she considered her answer. "I'm not sure how much I should tell you, Cade. It's very personal information."

"You might keep in mind that this time around I'm working for Miss Isabel," he said evenly.

"I know, but I'm not sure that having the wolf on our side changes the basic fact that he's still a predator. You must see that I'm walking a very fine line here. I'm responsible for supervising you. I realize I have to give you enough room to work. But I also have to be certain I don't do anything Miss Isabel wouldn't want done. I don't want to accidentally give you information that she might want kept confidential."

"If you want me to do a decent job, you can't tie my hands."

"That is, of course, a lovely rationale for turning you loose, but I don't think I'll buy it completely," she responded coolly. "I will try to answer your question, however. I don't want you claiming that I made it impossible for you to work at all. Miss Isabel wouldn't appreciate that."

"And you're determined to please Miss Isabel."

"She's my employer." Jamie shrugged with a nonchalance she didn't feel.

"For a while this summer you used to worry about pleasing me," Cade said quite deliberately.

"For a while this summer I lost my head," she retorted. "Working for Miss Isabel may not be quite as exciting as getting myself seduced by a professional business spy, but it has its compensations."

She knew a split second too late that she'd gone too far. Cade's hand moved so quickly that she couldn't have backed away in time to escape even if she had been warned. He reached across the counter, powerful fingers closing around her wrist, capturing her. His eyes blazed with temper.

"I am not a professional spy, damn it. I had my reasons for what I did this summer. I've explained them and I refuse to apologize for them. If you have any sense, Jamie Garland, you will learn to exercise a bit of caution. I'm aware that you're feeling vengeful, but there are limits, lady. Keep it in mind."

"Is this what you meant about doing things my way?" she dared, aware of the strength in his hand. He wasn't hurting her, but she knew she could never have broken the grip.

Abruptly he released her and picked up his coffee. Jamie could read the seething annoyance in him, but he was firmly tethered on the self-imposed leash. When he spoke again it was with extreme politeness. "I believe you were about to explain what you meant when you said Miss Isabel had 'not exactly' taken anything with her when she left Santa Barbara?"

Jamie blinked owlishly behind the lenses of her glasses, peering at him dubiously. Had he really backed down or was he tricking her? This was ridiculous. She had to have more faith in herself. She lounged against the counter, sipping coffee with great casualness. Damned if she would allow him to see how nervous he made her.

"There was a letter and a package," she began quietly.

"That she took with her?"

"No. Waiting for us here when we got home."

"Mailed or privately delivered?" Cade demanded.

"Mailed. It was waiting in the box when we got here." Jamie hesitated. "It was addressed to Miss Isabel. She opened it and told me it had been sent by Hadley. Mailed before he disappeared."

Cade was fully alert. "What was in the package?"

Jamie took another sip of coffee before admitting, "I don't know. Miss Isabel never told me. She said it was personal."

"I thought she shared just about everything with you."

"Normally she does, but you have to understand, Cade, she was very upset about her brother's death. Very depressed. She wasn't acting normally."

He thought about that. "So what happened to the contents of the package?"

"She took whatever it was and put it in my safe-deposit box at the bank in Carmel."

"Your safe-deposit box?" He looked astonished.

"I got it free when I opened the account at the bank," Jamie explained impatiently. "But since I never had anything all that valuable to put into it, I let Miss Isabel use it. We're both authorized to get into it. She never got around to getting one of her own. She doesn't like to be bothered with petty details. That's why she hired me in the first place, remember?"

Cade swore softly. "Whatever is in that package must have been important."

"I think it was something *personal*," Jamie stressed. "Something he wanted her to have. Don't you see? He must have known things were about to collapse. Perhaps he was already contemplating suicide at that point. In any event, he couldn't talk to his sister about it. He probably wrote something extremely personal by way of a farewell note to her and mailed it shortly before taking the boat out for the last time."

"Unless we can find out what's in that safe-deposit box, we'll never know for sure." Cade drummed his fingers lightly on the tiled counter.

"Don't look at me like that Cade. Miss Isabel *trusts* me with her personal affairs. I have earned that trust. I won't betray it." Jamie stood tensely on the other side of the counter, preparing herself to remain firm against what she knew was coming next.

"I'm not about to suggest that you betray her," Cade said quietly. "As I keep reminding you, I'm looking after Miss Isabel's interests these days. There might be information in that safe-deposit box that I could use to figure out for certain what happened to Fitzgerald. And it is your safe-deposit box, you said, not hers..."

Jamie shook her head stubbornly. "If there had been anything useful along those lines, Miss Isabel would have told me about it. I don't think she learned anything at all for certain about his fate from the contents of that package. If she had, she wouldn't have told me to go ahead and hire you, would she?"

"We won't know that until we see what's in the box," Cade shot back smoothly.

Jamie thought about the way Miss Isabel had handled the contents of the package from her brother. Never before had the older woman been so quiet and secretive. Whatever was in the envelope had obviously been of a deeply personal nature. It was equally obvious that it hadn't shed any light on Hadley's disappearance. If it had, Jamie felt certain Miss Isabel would have said something, or maybe she would have vetoed the idea of hiring Cade. No, at this point it was clear to Jamie where her duty lay. Miss Isabel did not want the contents of that package made public.

"I won't let you into the safe-deposit box, Cade."

"You don't trust me, do you? Not even an inch. What's the matter now? Do you think I'm still looking for more evidence to pin on Fitzgerald?"

"I have an obligation to look after Miss Isabel's interests. Whatever was in that package was obviously of a private nature."

"Most stuff that gets put into safe-deposit boxes is of a private nature," Cade growled. "That's precisely the reason I want to see whatever it was that Hadley sent to his sister. Jamie, I—"

"No, Cade."

For a moment a silent battle of wills raged over the breakfast counter, and then Cade moved his head in disgust. "You and your sense of loyalty. You're carrying it to extremes, Jamie."

"I don't see it that way."

"I wonder what the hell you'll do if you ever have to make a choice."

Her mouth tightened. "What kind of choice?"

"Never mind. Can I have another slice of that peanut-butter toast? It sticks so nicely to the roof of my mouth."

But she knew what he meant. He was wondering what she would do if she ever again had to choose between him and her sense of duty to Miss Isabel. Let him worry about her decision. It would keep him on his toes, Jamie decided. Besides, she couldn't have answered the question, anyway. She didn't know the answer. And she shied inwardly from examining the dangerous possibilities inherent in the problem.

Breakfast was finished in silence, somewhat sullen on Jamie's part, thoughtful on Cade's. When it was over, Jamie stiffly volunteered to show him her office. With a polite nod he stood aside, waiting for her to lead the way.

"I keep all of Miss Isabel's records in here," Jamie said as she flung open the door of the round room that served as her office. "Her tax information is in that file cabinet over there. I don't do the actual tax forms for her. I send them to her accountant. Records of the sales of her paintings are here in this drawer. The details on her various investments are all over there under the tax data." She swung around challengingly. "Anything else you want to know?"

Cade scanned the windowed room, examining the old-fashioned rolltop desk, the file cabinets and the array of plants that stood near the window. He shook his head. "This will make an interesting place to start. I don't suppose you have any journal or ledger? Some sort of index to everything that's in that file cabinet? A written record of her business transactions?"

She tilted her head, a trace of mockery in her small smile. "You mean you don't feel like going through every item in each drawer? I thought you were a thorough sort of investigator."

"I am," he said blandly, "but I also believe in doing things efficiently."

"How could I forget? I know all about your efficiency, don't I?" She turned away and opened one of the desk drawers. Withdrawing two notebooks, she set them on the desk. A pang of embarrassed uncertainty assailed her. "I guess you could call those a journal and a ledger."

"What do you mean, you 'guess'?" Idly he walked over to the desk and flipped open the cover of the top book. It revealed a page filled out in Jamie's slightly irregular handwriting.

Jamie's sense of embarrassment grew. She could feel the red flush staining her cheeks. "Well, you have to remember that when I first came to work for Miss Isabel I didn't have any formal training in this sort of thing. I, uh, majored in history in college, if you'll recall," she added with a humbleness that appalled her. Why on earth should she be apologizing to him for her unprofessional record-keeping systems?

"Even if you hadn't told me the knowledge wouldn't surprise me. I wouldn't have assumed you were the type to get a really practical education," he mused as he flipped through a few more pages of the notebook. "The journal is kept by the month?"

"I didn't know how else to start tracking things. Everything was in such a mess when I arrived two years ago. I talked to Miss Isabel's accountant, and he told me the kind of information he would need to keep her taxes straight. From there on I was on my own. I sort of made it up as I went along."

"You made up the details of her tax records?" Cade murmured interestedly.

Jamie's flush deepened. "Of course not. I meant I invented the record-keeping system. I didn't know anything about double-entry bookkeeping or account books or journals or ledgers. So I had to fake it. There's so much to keep track of," she went on, feeling pressed and growing slightly agitated under the pressure. Jamie waved a hand around the room. "Honestly, Cade, it's a big job. There are dealings with galleries, all this art-work that has to be kept inventoried, her personal finances. We're thinking of getting her incorporated, which will mean even more work. It goes on and on!"

"Another romantic, dreamy-eyed history major overwhelmed by reality." Cade grinned.

Jamie ignored that and stalked to the door. "Call me if you have any questions."

"Just one more thing."

"Yes?" She paused, glaring back at him over her shoulder.

"There's a desk in Miss Isabel's bedroom," Cade began slowly. "What does she keep in there?"

"Not much," Jamie said honestly. "Some personal correspondence, photographs, a few trinkets. Just odds and ends. She turned all the important financial stuff over to me when I arrived."

Cade nodded. "Okay. I'll have a look through it after I've gone over this stuff." He sat down at the roll-top desk and pulled the handwritten journal toward himself. It was apparent that he was immediately and completely absorbed in the task at hand.

Jamie hesitated and then decided that there was no way he could possibly get through the contents of her office before lunch. She would worry later about how much of Miss Isabel's personal correspondence to turn over to him. She walked out into the hall and stood there for a moment, fretting over what Cade would think about her unprofessional bookkeeping system.

It was ridiculous to be nervous or embarrassed. After all, she had done the best she could. Still, she had just left her poor, handwritten, unsophisticated records with a man whose business had once involved analyzing and tearing apart highly complex accounting systems. He was bound to find her unskilled attempts at record keeping rather laughable.

Well, there was nothing she could do about it now, Jamie told herself philosophically and went into the kitchen to get another cup of coffee. Then, feeling restless, she wandered out into the living room and picked up a volume she had been reading on the history of how the British had lost their American colonies.

But the foibles and follies and occasional acts of idealism that had characterized the eighteenth century failed to hold her attention this morning. She had her own foibles, follies and idealism with which to contend. Jamie realized she also had a lot of memories.

She found herself gazing out the window through the trees into the distance where the Pacific Ocean stretched forever. It was the same ocean that had extended into forever off the coast of Santa Barbara. This summer her dreams had extended into forever, too. Time had taken on curious properties during the two months she had known Cade Santerre. It had seemed to stop in some ways and in others it had appeared to be rushing past far too quickly. In its wake time had left images that were indelibly etched in her memory.

A few of those images returned to haunt her now just as they had haunted her steadily for the past six weeks. Sometimes it was the little things that seemed so vivid. She recalled the clasp of Cade's hand around her own as she had walked on the beach with him. His fingers contained such strength, and yet he had always touched her with a gentleness that had never failed to amaze her. The combination of power and tenderness in Cade had been deeply compelling. It was one of the reasons she had not been able to push him out of her mind during the past six weeks; one of the reasons she would never be able to forget him. Last night he had held her in his arms with that same enthralling combination of strength and gentleness. Jamie knew she was dangerously close to the brink of forever.

During the next few hours she tried very hard to read the book in her lap, but the words on the page wouldn't stay together in coherent sentences. Too many stray thoughts and memories intruded. She thought of Cade working in her study and wondered about his past. How could such a coolheaded, pragmatic man ever have walked away from a lucrative career in accounting in favor of the far more unpredictable life of a charter-boat captain?

Then her mind skipped along to scenes from Santa Barbara. Scenes that always involved Cade. Pâté and French bread shared on a secluded stretch of beach, an

afternoon spent wandering through the beautiful
Spanish mission together, a morning drive along the
coast. And always there were memories of the evenings spent talking over wine and good food. They
had talked about so many things, Jamie realized: the
history that she loved, the sailing that Cade enjoyed,
art, politics, their own personal philosophies. Jamie's
mouth twisted wryly. Everything under the California
sun except the truth had been discussed during those
two months in Santa Barbara. Cade had had priorities
that had precluded discussing that topic.

Priorities. Loyalties. Commitments.

The words tumbled around in her mind. She wasn't
the only one who was capable of feeling the pull of
such demands. For the first time Jamie allowed herself
to openly recognize that Cade, too, might have been
struggling with loyalties and commitments this summer. She thought about Cade's sister. Faced with a
similar situation, Jamie acknowledged, she might have
tried to walk the same line Cade had walked for two
months in Santa Barbara.

Then she remembered his comment at breakfast and
shivered. She hoped she would never have to choose
between her own loyalties.

Cade emerged a few minutes before noon, stretch-
ing hugely as he walked into the living room to find Jamie. She glanced up anxiously from the book she had
been trying to read.

"How did it go?" she asked cautiously.

"It was *interesting*." He nodded. "Yes, I think that's

the word. Interesting. You have a novel approach to the task of bookkeeping, Jamie."

"Never mind the cracks about my bookkeeping. Did you find anything useful?"

"Possibly." Cade sank down on the wicker lounge across from her, shoving his jeaned legs out in front of him. He laced his fingers behind his head and regarded her as if she were a specimen under a microscope. "Possibly not. Hard to know at this point. There are the names of some companies Fitzgerald dealt with that should be checked out. They might provide some leads." He paused. "Did I ever tell you just how much you can learn about a person by studying the way they keep track of financial matters?"

"You were not in that office to study me," she gritted.

"I know, but I couldn't help but pick up a few items of interest along the way. Actually I was quite impressed with your creativity at times. A case of '79 Bordeaux is a business expense?"

"Miss Isabel needs it for occasional artistic inspiration and I need it to get through the job of doing the monthly entries in that dumb journal."

"Four hundred dollars a month for petty cash?"

"I discovered it was easier to create a petty-cash fund rather than note down every itty-bitty little purchase in the journal," Jamie explained austerely. "Much more efficient."

"Fifty percent of the utilities written off as a business expense?"

"You can't expect Miss Isabel to paint in the dark!"

"A thousand-dollar television set put down as office furniture?"

"Miss Isabel is a great fan of soap operas," Jamie defended. "They give her a lot of creative ideas. Look, Cade, I didn't send you into that office to nitpick every little detail of my present record-keeping system. You were supposed to be looking for ways to track down Hadley!"

"It was a fascinating experience. I can't even begin to imagine the inventiveness a full-scale IRS audit might reveal. You have a really imaginative approach to bookkeeping, Jamie. A definite flair and style all your own. I told you record-keeping techniques are almost as unique to individuals as fingerprints." Tawny eyes gleamed with amusement.

"Did you learn anything about Hadley while you were snooping through my books?" Jamie asked in chilled tones.

"I learned that he kept his sister's investments conservative, as you said. I called Gallagher on your office phone, by the way."

"Did he have any news?"

"No. Just that there's been nothing yet to contradict the suicide theory. I asked him to check a couple of names on the board of directors of one of the real estate partnerships in which Fitzgerald had his sister invest. Thought I recognized at least one of them as a man who was distantly involved with Fitzgerald on a land-fraud scheme five years ago. It probably won't lead us anywhere useful." Again Cade stretched luxuriously. "What's for lunch?"

Jamie considered the matter along with her own tentative desire to understand this man better than she had this summer. "How about driving into Carmel? I know a couple of nice places there. Besides, I need some groceries. I only picked up a few things yesterday."

"Suits me." Cade got to his feet and reached for her hand. "Come along, my creative little accountant. We might as well eat, drink and be merry as long as we can, for tomorrow they may slap you in jail"

"Jail!" Horrified, Jamie dug in her heels and stared up at him.

"I'm only teasing you," Cade said, chuckling.

"Are you sure? Cade, I wasn't deliberately doing anything dishonest. I was only trying to interpret things to Miss Isabel's advantage. Everyone says you have to use every available loophole or else you wind up paying a lot of excess taxes."

"Stop worrying," he growled, propelling her out through the front door and into the waiting Mazda. "If worse comes to worst, I'll bake you a cake with a file in it."

"Cade!"

He slid in beside her, turned the key in the ignition and slanted her a strangely compelling glance. "Better be nice to me, honey. You may need my professional skills one of these days. I'm real good at finding loopholes."

"How much would you charge for keeping me out of trouble with the IRS?" Jamie grumbled as she fastened her seat belt.

"You'd be indebted to me for the rest of your life."

The outing to Carmel proved to be unexpectedly pleasant for Jamie. Cade seemed to be in a light-hearted, easygoing mood. He chatted casually with her over lunch in a tiny European-style café, offered to spend some time browsing through the myriad little boutiques that lined Carmel's quaint streets and generally made himself agreeable. Jamie wasn't quite sure how to interpret the good-naturedness, but she found herself taking advantage of it.

She took him into one of the local galleries where Miss Isabel had some work on display, and later they shared a cup of espresso. When it was finally time to leave the wealthy picturesque village of the sea, Jamie realized she had forgotten for a while just why she and Cade were again spending time together. The lovely afternoon was all too reminiscent of the many such days they had spent in Santa Barbara.

It was only as Cade guided the Mazda back along the narrow, curving highway hugging the cliff above the sea that Jamie questioned Cade's motives. She wouldn't put it past him to deliberately re-create a day that brought back warm memories of the time spent in Santa Barbara. She must be constantly on the alert, she told herself firmly. And then she realized that she had willingly participated in the fantasy that afternoon. She, too, wanted to re-create the feelings they had shared this summer. That way lay danger. The safest way to maintain the uneasy status quo was to keep everything on a business basis. For a while this afternoon she had neglected to do that. The reward for allowing her guard to slip had been a wonderful day spent with Cade.

"I've thought about letting you at Miss Isabel's private desk," she began as Cade pulled into the drive in front of the house.

"Have you?" He didn't seem unduly concerned.

"I think it would be all right. I don't know if there's anything useful to be found there, but I don't believe she'd mind if you had a look."

"I'll do it in the morning."

She slanted him a quick glance. "Not this evening?"

"Morning will be soon enough."

"Oh."

"Now about this evening," he went on imperturbably as he climbed out of the car.

"What about it?"

"I was going to suggest we examine the details of one of those business expenses of yours."

Jamie eyed him uneasily as she followed him to the door.

"Which expense?"

"The '79 Bordeaux."

"You don't think it's a legitimate deduction?"

"I suspect I'll have to sample a bottle or two in order to determine that."

"Ah, I see," Jamie said sweetly. "I'll bring one up from the cellar. You can open the smoked oysters."

"Yes, ma'am."

Cade's good mood lasted through the dinner of tortellini, salad and crusty bread. It took two bottles of the '79 Bordeaux to determine its legitimacy as a business expense, but in the end Cade agreed with Jamie that it did, indeed, inspire creativity.

It wasn't until the dishes had been washed that Jamie began to wonder how she would handle the rest of the evening. There had been no pressure from Cade, but it would soon be time to go to bed and she had to be prepared to deal with the inevitable confrontation.

She would be polite but firm, she told herself.

She would assert her control over the situation by making certain he knew he would sleep alone.

She would maintain the friendly atmosphere without allowing it to become intimate.

Jamie was adding to the list, fine-tuning her proposed responses in preparation for the moment Cade would make his move, when she happened to step into her office. She was on her way down the hall to the bathroom at the time and simply decided to have a look inside.

It was curiosity as much as anything else that made her want to see how the place looked after Cade had been through it with a fine-tooth comb.

She discovered that it appeared almost distractingly neat. The excessively pristine condition of all the papers and records on the shelves made her wander over to the desk and glance inside a drawer. Jamie couldn't help wondering how far Cade's inclination to tidy things up had gone.

The first thing she noticed was that the envelope of

keys that she kept in the top desk drawer had been opened. She always kept it sealed.

For a long moment she simply stood there, contemplating the full meaning of the small change in her office environment. She didn't have to dump the packet of keys onto the desk top to confirm what she already had begun to suspect.

The safe-deposit-box key was missing. Jamie chilled.

Hardly surprising, she thought sadly. After all, she had been fool enough to leave Cade alone in her office all morning. He'd had ample opportunity to examine the keys in the envelope. Safe-deposit-box keys were distinctive things. Easy to identify and remove from a pile. Cade wouldn't have had any trouble selecting it and pocketing it.

SEVEN

Perhaps Cade hadn't taken the key. Perhaps she had misplaced it. After all, it had been ages since she'd needed it. The last time she had actually seen the safe-deposit-box key was the day she had taken some of Miss Isabel's insurance policies down to the bank for her. That had been months ago. Isabel had used the extra key Jamie had once given her when she'd put Hadley's package in the vault.

Besides, Jamie thought desperately as she lay wide awake in Miss Isabel's bed, what good was the key without an authorized signature to go with it? You had to sign to get into the vault at the bank. Or did a smart investigative accountant with government contacts know how to get around that barrier? If Cade showed up at the bank with the proper key and some sort of government clearance he might be able to get into the box. Jamie just didn't know.

Whether or not he could pull off that trick didn't bother her nearly as much as the possibility of his having taken the key in the first place. As she lay staring at the dancing shadows on the ceiling, Jamie realized the real problem.

She didn't want to believe he was capable of that kind of deceit.

What an idiot she was. Jamie reminded herself grimly that she'd had proof enough of his unscrupulous tactics this summer. If Cade Santerre wanted something, he didn't let anything stand in his way.

But she had spent the past six weeks making excuses for him, telling herself that he'd had his reasons for what he'd done. She'd even begun to believe the evidence against Hadley, although she had been careful not to voice such traitorous thoughts to Miss Isabel. Jamie didn't even want to think about the nights she had lain awake dreaming various and sundry ways of confronting Cade again. The notion of using him to verify Hadley's death had seemed a stroke of genius at the time. The perfect way for Jamie to give Cade another chance without dragging her own pride through the mud a second time.

"He knows more about Hadley than anyone else except yourself, Miss Isabel," Jamie had reasoned when she presented the idea to her employer. "What's more, he's got all sorts of contacts with various authorities. If anyone could find out for certain what happened to your brother, it would be Cade."

"But he must hate poor Hadley!" Miss Isabel had protested.

"Not necessarily. Someone hired Cade to do a job and he did it. I think it's as simple as that. We could hire him ourselves and if he accepts, I think he'll do what we want him to do. I believe he's something of a, uh, professional in his own way."

"Do you really think he could tell us anything more about my brother?"

Jamie regarded her employer with compassion. "I think he might be able to set your mind at ease by verifying the facts."

"If I knew for certain he was dead, I could cope with the knowledge," Miss Isabel had admitted softly. "It's just that I have the oddest sensation that he is alive. I won't be able to rest until I can be sure."

"I understand."

"I always liked Mr. Santerre. He seemed like such a nice man. Even at the end he seemed to be worried about you and me. Perhaps he was just doing a job and sincerely regretted having to hurt us in the process. Do you think Mr. Santerre would accept an offer of employment from us?" There was a flicker of hope in Miss Isabel's eyes. "After everything that happened this summer?"

"I'm not sure. But I think it's possible."

Jamie hadn't known why she thought it was possible. It was just that, like her employer, she had a restless feeling of her own. It had nothing to do with Hadley Fitzgerald, but she couldn't rest until she'd satisfied herself that Cade's motives this summer hadn't been as deceitful as she'd believed. His final words as he'd left the Fitzgerald home in Santa Barbara still rang in her ears. He was waiting for her. All she had to do was to go and find him.

Now, as she faced the prospect of his having stolen the safe-deposit-box key, Jamie realized just how much hope she had been living with for the past six weeks. He must have taken it, she told herself for the fiftieth time.

But it was just barely possible she herself had lost it. There was even the off chance that Miss Isabel had taken Jamie's key instead of her own the day she had driven into Carmel with that package from Hadley.

The other possibilities didn't change the fact that the most likely one was that Cade had simply come across the key this morning while going through Jamie's desk and helped himself. He certainly had been in a good mood for the rest of the day, she thought resentfully. She didn't want to believe it was because he'd gotten what he'd wanted. This afternoon had been a romantic fantasy, a re-creation of the magic that had existed this summer. It would be unbearable if the hours of happiness had existed simply because Cade had gotten hold of the damn safe-deposit-box key.

If only she knew for certain what was going through his mind! Jamie turned onto her side, eyes wide open in the darkness. She was behaving like some sort of silly moth around a flame again; wary, but drawn toward the fire in spite of all the logical reasons why she should flee. She felt torn by the separate but powerful forces operating on her. Love and the dangerously reckless emotional commitment she felt toward Cade were at war with logic and evidence.

Desperately she tried to decide what motives Cade might have for taking the key. He could be looking for further information on Hadley, with the intention of turning it over to the authorities. He might simply be governed by his own determined curiosity and his decision to do the job for which he'd been hired. There was a relentless streak in him that Jamie knew well. And he didn't appreciate anyone standing in his path the way she had today when she'd refused him access to the box.

It was conceivable he had taken the key because he felt that whatever was in the safe-deposit box would help him complete his task. The task for which Jamie herself had hired him. There were definite risks in hiring predators. They tended to do things in their own way.

She was dwelling on that bit of wisdom when the door to the bedroom opened. There was no light from the hall to illuminate Cade but his presence in the room was unmistakable. Jamie felt it in all her senses. She lay very still in the darkness and wondered what to do next.

"Jamie?" Cade came toward the bed, moving silently across the carpet.

Jamie sensed his approach and a very primitive part of her urged her to run. Another part of her whispered that there were answers to all her questions and that the only thing that counted tonight was the chance to spend another night in Cade's arms.

"You...you shouldn't be here, Cade." She didn't like the tremor in her voice, but she couldn't seem to control it.

"Where else would I be?" he asked gently, dropping

to one knee beside the bed and reaching out to touch the side of her face. In the shadows his tawny eyes seemed deep and beguilingly dark. "Why did you disappear tonight? Hasn't the day been good? Just like the days we used to spend in Santa Barbara. Why did you leave so abruptly? I've been sitting alone by myself wondering what I did wrong. Please, Jamie, tell me. Whatever it is, I'm sorry. I would sell my soul not to ruin things between us tonight."

Jamie swallowed, wanting to turn her lips into the palm of his hand as he stroked her. "It was late. We were up very early this morning, and I was tired."

"I'm tired, too," he murmured, his strong, blunt fingers trailing down the line of her throat. "I came to ask if I could sleep in your arms."

"Oh, Cade," she whispered starkly, "don't do this to me."

"Don't do what? Tell you that I want you? That I need you? That I've spent the past six weeks dreaming about holding you again? Jamie, I felt that I'd finally emerged from a cave last night. It's as though I've spent those six weeks in darkness. I'm so hungry for you, sweetheart. I don't want to push you. I swear I won't. Just let me crawl into bed beside you and hold you for a while."

The words were honey and fire, pouring over Jamie until she trembled. This was the man she had fallen in love with this summer and here he was, pleading for her tonight. Surely her instincts could not have been totally wrong about him. He was right: the day had been similar to one of those magic days of their summer. And she longed to recapture that magic completely.

"I wish I knew you better, Cade. I wish I knew how you think," she said wistfully. *Then, perhaps, I could learn to trust you completely again,* she added silently.

"All I can think about at the moment is you."

"And what were you thinking of earlier today?"

"You. In one way or another, you've been on my mind since the moment we met. Last night you let me make love to you. Jamie, I'll give you anything you ask if you'll let me make love to you again tonight."

She caught her breath. "The truth, Cade? Will you give me the truth?"

The hardening of his features was barely visible in the darkness, but Jamie sensed it. "What truth do you want, honey? The truth about the way I feel? That's easy enough to give you. I'm on fire for you. I want nothing more than to take that two hundred-and-ninety-seven-dollar nightgown off you and dump it on the floor."

"I thought you only wanted to crawl into bed and hold me."

"I'll take whatever you choose to give. No more, no less. I won't push you into giving me more than you can, Jamie."

"You sound very humble tonight, Cade. I don't think I've ever heard you sound quite that way before," she murmured wonderingly.

"When a man is on his knees begging a woman for anything she cares to give, he's bound to sound a little humble. Jamie, please. Trust me, sweetheart." His hand moved to her shoulder, and the heat of it sank through the fabric of the expensive French nightgown, warming Jamie.

All of her own inner warnings grew mute. Jamie realized on some distant level that she was being captivated by this new side of Cade's personality. He wasn't demanding anything from her; rather he was pleading. It gave her a sense of safety, a sense of being in command of the potentially dangerous situation.

"Cade, are you really here only because of me?"

"Don't you know the answer to that yet?" He leaned close and brushed his mouth against hers. "Please, Jamie. I want you so..."

The soft caress unraveled the last barriers. She wanted this man; more than that she still loved him. Jamie had learned the hard way that becoming involved with him was risky, but tonight there was something new to be considered. Cade was no longer the seducer. Tonight he was begging to be seduced.

Jamie looked up at him through her lashes and silently held out her arms.

"Jamie, honey...!"

He came down beside her in a fierce but carefully restrained rush. She realized he was still wearing his jeans, but that was all. When he gathered her into his arms she kissed the bare skin of his smoothly muscled chest, delighting in the hard, sure feel of him. Cade's husky groan of response sent a shiver of pleasure through Jamie.

"I've got to get out of these damn jeans," Cade muttered, his hand going to his zipper.

"I'll get you out of them." Jamie rose to her knees. "Just lie still, Cade. I'll undress you." Her own gentle aggression was a new source of excitement to her. She felt wonderfully wanton and free and uninhibited. She also felt strangely secure.

That sense of security increased as Cade meekly allowed her to tug the denims down his lean hips. His hands moved through the auburn tumble of her hair as she worked at the task of undressing him. And when she leaned forward to drop a warm, damp kiss on his thigh, the fingers in her hair went tense with masculine excitement.

"Jamie, you must know by now that you have the power to drive me crazy. Oh, God, honey, I'm burning up. I don't know how I lasted six weeks without you!"

His arousal fascinated Jamie and sent an answering response flickering through her veins. Her obvious power over him was a heady thing, leading her faster and faster down the paths of desire. When Cade's hands dropped from her hair to the flimsy fastenings of her nightgown, she barely noticed.

Her own hands moved with delicate tantalizing rhythms, gliding along Cade's hard thighs, holding him intimately until he groaned aloud. When she caught his flat male nipple between her teeth, he ground out her name in tones of aching need. With growing excitement Jamie continued to torment and tease. Glorying in the level of passion she was invoking, she gave herself up to playing the role of seductress. Finally Cade's hoarse pleas and her own desire overcame her fascination with the enthralling new game she had been playing.

"Please, Jamie. I can't take much more. Come and take me, honey. *Take me!*"

It came as a distant surprise to Jamie to discover that she was no longer wearing her nightgown. She couldn't remember taking it off. Not that it mattered. All she wanted now was to complete the lovemaking. She wanted to bring Cade to shuddering fulfillment and know that she was the cause of that fulfillment.

She flowed over his strength, fitting her soft, womanly body to his with a slow impact that made both of them suck air into their lungs. Her nails bit deeply into his shoulders as she sat boldly astride him, absorbing his power into herself. Cade's palms lifted to cup the soft weight of her breasts, and his eyes gleamed with hunger.

"You're a witch," he breathed as he felt the tight warmth of her body surrounding him. "A sweet, fiery, passionate little witch who doesn't yet know her own power. But you will after tonight, won't you, sweetheart? You'll be sure of both of us by morning."

He was right, she decided exultantly as she began to move against him. Always before he had been the one in control of the lovemaking. Cade was the one who had teased and seduced her this summer. He was the one who had taken the lead last night, sweeping her up and carrying her to bed. But tonight everything was reversed, and Jamie was suddenly and vividly aware of her own power over this man. For the first time she felt truly confident of it.

The knowledge drove her up a spiral of excitement that thrilled her. Cade was swept along with her. His hands were on Jamie's hips, holding her tautly as she guided them both to the heights. Again and again he lifted himself in obedient, eager response to her feminine demands, until with a startled cry Jamie felt herself tighten in unbearable pleasure. Then she was shivering violently, collapsing against his chest even as he called her name and shuddered deeply.

"Jamie, Jamie, my sweet Jamie..." The big hands moved on her body in slow, soothing motions as Cade cradled the soft, limp weight of the woman who lay along his length.

She was so full of fire and passion when she let herself go, he thought wonderingly. He would never get his fill of her. He had been needing her so, and it was infinitely reassuring to know that she needed him. It was also very satisfying to see the feminine pride and sureness come to the surface tonight. It had been touch and go there for a while this evening. He had been certain that she was relaxing around him earlier today, and dinner had been reminiscent of the evenings out they had spent in Santa Barbara. A good sign. Everything had seemed to be on track until an hour ago when her mood had suddenly altered, and she had disappeared into the bedroom.

Cade had been dismayed and annoyed. He had been so sure he was recovering all the ground he had lost: sure that when it was time to go to bed tonight she would follow him without any qualms.

But again he had miscalculated. It was astonishing

to Cade that he did that so damn frequently with Jamie. He seldom made such mistakes with other people.

So once more he had been forced to take a new tack. As he had lounged broodingly in the living room, realizing that Jamie had gone to bed without him, he had finally decided to try the humble approach. Maybe if she were more confident of her power over him, she would not be so wary. It had been worth a try.

The experiment had some unexpected side effects, Cade thought in wry amusement as he toyed with a strand of Jamie's hair. He had gotten a surprising degree of satisfaction out of the sensual game. Accustomed to being the aggressor, he hadn't realized how much pleasure there was in having a woman take the lead. Maybe he'd try it again sometime. But meanwhile, he decided in unmitigated relief, his tactics appeared to have achieved a large measure of success. Aware of a pleasantly lethargic feeling of sensual satisfaction, he noted that the success was on several levels. Being around Jamie had that effect on him. He always seemed to be aware of her on more than one level at a time.

He felt Jamie stir in his arms, and he smiled down into her heavy-lidded eyes. She was cute without her glasses, he thought. The gray-green eyes were always so intent, so very serious as she tried to focus clearly.

Jamie saw the satisfied amusement in the curve of his mouth, and she hoped she hadn't played the fool once more. He had responded to her, she reminded herself. She had led and he had followed willingly, making no secret of his need. She had been in control. She must remain in control now. She must get some answers, or she would go out of her mind.

"There's something I have to know, Cade."

"Ask," he ordered easily, bending down to nuzzle the hollow of her throat.

Jamie touched his hair. He felt heavy and deeply relaxed as he lay against her. His bare feet were tangled intimately with her own. Jamie realized she was afraid to ask her question. But she had to know the truth. Closing her eyes, she forced out the words.

"Did you take the safe-deposit-box key in my desk out of its envelope this morning?" she managed in a rush.

Instantly the languid male relaxation in him vanished. Cade stiffened, lifting his head again to meet her eyes. "What did you say?"

She licked her lips nervously and opened her eyes. But Jamie refused to retreat. "You heard me. The safe-deposit-box key that was in my desk is missing. I know you wanted to get your hands on it. So I'm asking if you took it."

He looked dumbfounded at first and then, with menacing swiftness, glittering anger lit his eyes. "You're saying I stole that damn key?"

"I'm asking," she emphasized desperately, beginning to wish she'd chosen a more opportune time. Then again, how did a woman find an opportune time to ask a man if he'd stolen from her?

"You're accusing me of theft?" Cade sat up abruptly. "I don't believe it! After making love to me like that? How the hell can you turn around and accuse me of stealing from you?"

"I'm not accusing you!" she gasped, inching toward the side of the bed. "I went into my office this evening and found the key was missing. You spent the whole morning in that office going through everything. And you had been angry because I refused to open the safe-deposit box for you."

"So you assumed that because the key is now missing, I took it!" Cade surged to his feet beside the bed and stood glowering down at her. The rage in him was plain.

"I'm just asking for the truth," Jamie countered, torn between wariness and a rising sense of anger. "Is that too much? I won't have you playing games with me, Cade. You played one too many this summer. You're working for me now, and if you won't be honest with me I'll fire you!"

"I'm working for Miss Isabel!" he shot back tightly. "I'm in charge!"

"The hell you are! I will tell you one thing, however. I did not steal the damn key. Show me where it was supposed to be in your desk."

"Believe me, it's gone," she muttered.

"Show me!"

"All right, I will!" Furiously she slid from the bed, grabbing for her glasses and then her nightgown, which she slid quickly over her head. Then, the soft fabric floating behind her, she led the way down the hall to her desk. A few minutes later she yanked open the drawer and displayed the torn packet of keys. "See? It's gone."

"What does the key look like?" Cade dumped out the remaining keys and flipped through them quickly.

"Like a safe-deposit-box key!"

"You're sure it's not one of these?"

"Yes, I'm sure. Miss Isabel has one just like it. I can show you what it looks like, but I don't see why—"

"Let's have a look," he interrupted bluntly.

"But Cade...!"

"I said, let's have a look," he bit out savagely.

Jamie spun around and again led the way back down the curving hall. Throwing on the light switch in Miss Isabel's room, she went over to the delicate-looking desk and wrenched open a drawer. Quickly she rummaged around until she found the velvet-lined tray in which Miss Isabel kept important keys. Triumphantly Jamie flung open the lid. Then her eyes widened in shock.

"Oh, no," she breathed.

Cade peered into the tray. "So? Which one is the safe-deposit-box key?"

"It's gone," Jamie said weakly. Startled and dismayed, she glanced up to find Cade watching her through narrowed eyes.

"Are you accusing me of taking this one, too?" he asked dangerously.

"No...I, that is, you couldn't have known about this one. And you haven't had a chance to go through Miss Isabel's desk yet. Cade, I...I don't understand..."

"You have got a problem, haven't you? Both keys

are missing, and you can't link me to the second theft, which means you have to ask some serious questions about the first. Careful, Jamie. You're going to get all tangled up in your own idiotic logic." He turned on his heel, scooped up his jeans from the floor and started out the door.

"Wait!" she called anxiously. "Where are you going?"

"Back to my own room," he said without bothering to glance over his shoulder. "I'll leave you alone to work on your little puzzle. Let me know if you come to any brilliant conclusions."

His scathing words echoed in Jamie's ears as she sank down onto one of the curved chairs beneath the painting of Hadley Fitzgerald. He was furious, she realized. And apparently with good reason. She sighed and looked down at the velvet tray she still clutched in one hand. All things considered, she was inclined to believe his protestations of innocence.

All things considered, of course, probably meant that she was a woman in love and would seize any excuse that exonerated her lover. But in this instance there did appear to be some fairly hard evidence in his favor. Thank God.

Mouth twisting wryly, Jamie tossed the small tray onto an end table and sat huddled in the chair, staring at nothing. She hadn't accused him of taking the key, she tried to reassure herself. She had only asked for the truth. She had grounds for questioning his actions. It wasn't as though he had never done anything to make her wonder about his scruples.

No, that wasn't completely fair. She might not have approved of his actions this summer, but she was forced to respect his reasons. Everyone had his or her own loyalties. Jamie's had been firmly with Miss Isabel and therefore, to a certain extent, with Miss Isabel's brother. Cade's loyalties, understandably enough, had been with his sister and brother-in-law. Jamie had been unlucky enough to get in the middle. And when all was said and done, Cade had tried to get her clear before the authorities moved in on Hadley. She didn't doubt his intentions. On the other hand, she didn't like being manipulated, either. Cade was a master at that sort of thing.

But she loved him. That was the bitter irony that lay at the bottom of this whole mess. She loved him and she wanted him to love her.

Could a man who was accustomed to always being in control, whose instincts about people were so good that he could analyze and assess and manipulate them with consummate ease, ever really be able to love, Jamie wondered. The next question was whether or not she could ever completely trust such a man. Even when he claimed to be acting in her best interests, he tended to do things his own way, without bothering to consult her. He certainly hadn't bothered to explain the real reason he wanted her to take an unplanned vacation with him this summer. Probably because he had known she would have felt obliged to warn Miss Isabel about what was going to happen, Jamie acknowledged.

Loyalties. She and Cade had been caught in a set of

conflicting loyalties. Perhaps in his mind he'd had no choice but to handle her the way he had; not if he wanted to offer her some protection from the impending disaster. A part of her did not doubt that had been his intention.

None of that changed the facts. She had perfectly adequate reasons to be cautious around him. And she had not actually accused him of stealing the safe-deposit-box key, Jamie told herself once again. She had merely asked for the truth. He had been enraged at her lack of trust.

It was all very confusing, Jamie decided wearily, and it didn't answer the immediate questions. What had happened to the safe-deposit-box keys if Cade hadn't confiscated them? It didn't make any sense that Miss Isabel would have taken them with her on the cruise. She could have no possible use for them. Besides, she probably would have mentioned the fact to Jamie if she had decided to take them. The missing keys made that last letter from Hadley Fitzgerald more mysterious than ever.

"Hadley, what were you up to there at the last?" Jamie asked aloud, glancing at the painting. Hadley's aristocratic, gentlemanly features stared back at her. He looked every inch the successful, ethical businessman of the old school. The kind of man who took grave care of his sister's financial investments. And then promptly turned around and fleeced others without a moment's hesitation.

Jamie continued to stare at the man in the painting, remembering her nightmare in which there had seemed to be two Hadleys. The thick globs of paint and assorted artifacts that surrounded the central figure caught her attention. Miss Isabel had achieved a very interesting effect by including bits and pieces of Hadley's life in the final painting.

Jamie found herself staring even more intently at the picture, examining it in far greater detail than she'd bothered to do before. The bits and pieces that Miss Isabel had mired in the paint included a wide variety of ordinary objects.

Jamie took a deep breath and stared harder. Ordinary objects, all of them. Papers, pencils, part of a watch. There was even a small bit of metal poking out of one glob of acrylic, a bit of metal that resembled the tip of a key.

Across the hall in his own room, Cade paced the floor, scowling. She still didn't trust him. He couldn't believe it. The knowledge alternately enraged him and frightened him. Cade could understand the first emotion. The last perplexed him. He couldn't recall ever being this fundamentally nervous. He'd certainly known certain kinds of fear. There had been moments at sea that had a way of impressing upon a man that life was an extremely precarious thing, for example.

But this fear was of a different kind. It stemmed from a panicky feeling that Jamie might be slipping away from him. He had been so sure of Jamie at every step along the way, and at the last minute she always succeeded in surprising him. Why he couldn't calculate and control her actions the way he normally did other people's, Cade couldn't understand. It left him extremely worried. More than that, it left him strangely insecure. It also left him mad.

She had a lot of nerve accusing him of stealing that key. Who did she think she was to level a charge of outright dishonesty against him? And after he'd taken such care to give her a dose of feminine self-confidence this evening, too! He'd been trying so hard all day to reassure her and remind her of how good it had been between them in the summer. He'd been intent on rebuilding the relationship, and he'd thought he was making great progress until a few minutes ago.

The realization that her distrust of him went very deep was shattering. Cade sat down on the foot of the bed and locked his hands together in a fist as he thought about the subject. It was Miss Isabel's fault, he decided grimly. Somehow the older woman had established a bond of loyalty that kept getting in the way of Cade's efforts to establish his own bonds. Sweet, charming, brilliantly creative Miss Isabel. A woman who had obviously played the role of confidante, friend and mentor to Jamie for the past two years. Tough competition.

He had time, Cade reminded himself. He mustn't get panicked at this stage. Things weren't going as smoothly as he'd hoped, but he had time. Perhaps he had pushed too quickly tonight. Maybe the smart thing to do now was simply to keep at the job for which he'd been hired. *Take things one step at a time, Santerre.*

The problem, of course, was that he really had very little interest in working on the task of proving Fitzgerald dead. For one thing, he was reasonably convinced that the man had, indeed, committed suicide. A number of other men before him had done so when faced with ruin and scandal. Trying to prove otherwise seemed a pointless waste of time. Gallagher had assured him that the authorities were sure of their facts. But the job served to keep him near Jamie while he tried to unravel the twisted threads of her distrust and wariness.

There were one or two small matters he'd like to settle, just out of curiosity. He'd give a great deal to know what had been in that last package from Hadley, and he'd be very interested to discover exactly what had happened to the missing safe-deposit-box keys.

The keys. Cade focused on that element of the problem with abrupt attention. Yes, the questions surrounding them needed answers because they were so closely related to the questions concerning Fitzgerald's last letter.

The trouble was, Cade knew, he didn't stand much chance of getting his answers until he'd won Jamie's confidence again. He swore savagely. In that moment he could have strangled Hadley Fitzgerald and said some extremely unkind things to Isabel. Both of them seemed to be standing in the path that led to Jamie.

Cade got to his feet with sudden decision. First things first, he reminded himself. He had a job to do. In three long strides he reached the door and pulled it open. Then he padded softly across the hall to the room Jamie was using. Determinedly he flung open the door.

"Jamie, I know you're feeling hostile, resentful and generally uncooperative," he began roughly, "but that doesn't change the fact that I'm supposed to be working on a problem for Miss Isabel. We're going to have to cooperate with each other. And that means we're going to have to sit down and discuss a few matters."

She swung around as he entered the room, a small frown indicating the intensity with which she had been studying the portrait of Hadley Fitzgerald.

"I shouldn't have asked if you'd taken the key from my desk," she said in an odd little voice.

Cade eyed her narrowly. "That's nice to hear," he retorted sarcastically. "Mind telling me what gave you that bit of insight?"

She shook her head slowly. "You couldn't have taken that nor the one in Miss Isabel's desk, either."

"What makes you so sure?"

"I've found them."

That startled him. "Where?"

She glanced back at the picture on the wall. "Miss Isabel painted them into the portrait of Hadley. Why do you suppose she'd do that, Cade?"

Cade stared at the portrait as his analytical mind finally went to work. *About time you started thinking, Santerre,* he told himself in disgust.

"I don't think," he stated succinctly, "that there are any good reasons why she would do that. Only unpleasant ones."

EIGHT

"I was afraid you were going to say something along those lines." Jamie walked over to the closet to find a robe. The action was out of a need to give herself time to think as much as a desire to shield herself from Cade's hard, brilliant gaze. She had the awful sensation that everything was closing in on her, seeking to trap her and force her into confronting her loyalties. Soon she would be forced to make a decision that would take her perilously close to the borders of her duty to Miss Isabel. A sudden premonition assailed her that she might actually have to cross the border of loyalty entirely. She pushed the feeling aside.

"Jamie, you must realize now that we've got to find out what's in that safe-deposit box." Cade stood unyieldingly in the center of the room. It didn't take any unusual degree of perception to realize he'd made up his mind.

Jamie refused to meet his eyes as she tied the sash of the robe and walked slowly back to face the painting. "I don't understand, Cade. She finished that portrait the day before she left on the cruise. She didn't say anything about the keys or why she would make them a part of the picture. Why did she do it?''

"The answer is obvious," Cade said flatly. "She wanted to hide the keys."

"Because she didn't want anyone going into that box at the bank while she was gone," Jamie concluded bleakly. "She didn't trust me to protect her interests."

Cade moved, taking a step forward. His powerful hands settled on Jamie's shoulders. "Probably because whatever is in that letter from Hadley is very explosive or very incriminating. Jamie, this puts a whole new light on a couple of things."

"Such as?" she challenged, not liking the direction in which she saw herself heading. Unfortunately she didn't see any alternative.

"Such as your thinking you might have seen Fitzgerald at that gas station." Cade's voice hardened. "It makes me wonder just how your terrace door got opened last night. It also makes me wonder if perhaps you weren't having a bad dream or a case of double vision when you thought you saw the portrait move."

Jamie flinched. "You don't believe Hadley was in this room prowling around, do you?"

"I don't know what to believe at this point."

"Oh, my God." The thought staggered her.

"I'm not saying he was in here, but we can't take any more chances, honey. You must see that. We've got to find out what it is that Miss Isabel took such care to hide. Until we know what's in that last letter from

Fitzgerald, we're working blind. That could be very dangerous."

"Dangerous! Why should it be dangerous? Hadley was never involved in anything violent. He was a businessman. Even if he was mixed up in some shady deals they were *business* deals, not...not armed robbery or murder, for heaven's sake!"

Cade's mouth curved sardonically. "What you don't seem to understand, my naive, loyal little personal assistant, is that when the money is as big as it was in most of Fitzgerald's deals, you can't make any assumptions about how far someone would go to protect himself. People have been known to commit murder for a good deal less than even the smallest of one of Hadley Fitzgerald's transactions."

"You're saying Hadley is a murderer?" Jamie yelped.

"Jamie, I'm not saying anything for certain at this point except that we have to find out what we're dealing with before we get caught in something dangerous. Already there's a possibility that someone might have entered your room."

"We don't know that for certain. It could have been a dream," Jamie protested.

"I want a look at the contents of that package."

"That's all you've wanted since I mentioned it. A real single-track mind. I always said you were a thorough man," she muttered, pulling free of his grasp.

Cade watched her in cold silence for a moment before saying quietly, "If you won't let me have a look at whatever it was Miss Isabel stashed in that safe-deposit box, then I'm going to have to take you away from here."

Her head came around abruptly, eyes widening in shock. "Take me away! What on earth are you talking about? This is my home!"

"This is not your home, damn it. This is your place of employment and I have reason to believe that the working conditions may no longer be safe!"

"I'm not going to let you bully me into opening that safe-deposit box for you. The only thing you want is a look at that letter so you can satisfy your own curiosity!"

"Jamie, that's not true. You once admitted I've got good instincts when it comes to figuring out other people's motives and actions. Well, those instincts are in full sail right now and they're all telling me this whole scene is very big trouble. You never knew the side of Hadley Fitzgerald I uncovered. He was an unscrupulous man who didn't care one bit whom he hurt as long as the take was big. If he hasn't actually been involved in violence up to this point, it's probably only because violence hasn't been necessary. It doesn't mean he's not capable of it."

"You're talking as if he might still be alive."

"The possibility exists. Gallagher found nothing but an empty boat, remember. People have faked suicides before."

Jamie felt the pressure increasing. The trap was closing on her. Desperately she fought to keep her options open, struggling to avoid being pushed against the wall and forced to make a choice. Hands laced tightly in her lap, she sat down at the foot of the bed and tried to think.

"Miss Isabel believes so strongly that her brother is still alive," Jamie murmured aloud. "She just couldn't accept the evidence of his death."

"Perhaps her instincts were valid," Cade offered softly. "Jamie, she hired me to find out the truth. Whatever is in that safe-deposit box might give us the truth. I have to see that package."

"If it leads you to the conclusion that Hadley is still alive, you'll go straight back to your friend Gallagher with the information, won't you?" Jamie charged.

Cade hesitated before saying cautiously, "It's the logical thing to do."

"I knew it! That would hardly be what Miss Isabel would want and you're supposed to be working on her behalf."

"Look at it this way," Cade said, trying to reason with her. "If he is still alive, presumably he has the sense to stay out of the country. He's safe as long as he does that. If I can prove he's alive and figure out where he's living, Miss Isabel can contact him."

"But what if he's not safely out of the country?" Jamie said wildly. "What if he's here? What if it was him I saw the other day?"

"And what if it was him in your room last night? Then the situation is dangerous." Cade spoke coldly and deliberately. "You must see that, Jamie. I'll have to act. If I can't settle the issue by getting into that safe-deposit box, then I'll have to take you away from here in order to be sure of your safety."

"You don't have a right to make such arbitrary decisions where I'm concerned, Cade Santerre."

"I'm your lover," he stated uncompromisingly. "I have the right to protect you."

"Even if I don't want that protection?" she mocked angrily.

"Even if you're letting your sense of duty blind you to the danger in which you're involved. Yes."

"I still don't think there's any danger," she retorted. His overpowering certainty that he had the right to dictate her actions angered her. It also made her extremely nervous. She wasn't quite sure she could fight and win if it came to all-out war with Cade.

"That's because you don't want to acknowledge the possibility. Just as you're afraid to acknowledge that I'm your lover," Cade said almost gently. "Honey, you have a real knack for ignoring the obvious when it conflicts with the way you think the world should be. But I'm not going to let you go on ignoring the obvious much longer. There are too many risks involved."

"You can't force me to leave here," she flared.

"Are you going to stand there and tell me that you'd have no qualms at all now about staying in this house alone? That you wouldn't lie awake nights wondering why Miss Isabel hid your key as well as her own in that portrait? That every time you found a door or a window open you wouldn't wonder if someone had been prowling through the house? Come on, Jamie. You're inclined to be naive, but you're not exactly stupid. Furthermore, one of your talents is a very active imagination. Do you really want me to leave you alone? Maybe I should do exactly that. Why the hell am I banging my head against a brick wall? There are easier ways to get a headache."

She stared at him and realized that it had not occurred to her that Cade would leave her alone here. Somehow she had assumed he would remain in the vicinity now that questions had been raised. She had been subconsciously counting on his presence ever since she had seen the tips of the keys buried in the portrait. Some elemental instinct had told her that he wouldn't leave her alone with the mystery. Miss Isabel's house suddenly seemed isolated and huge. It no longer seemed like a home. Homes were places that held no unanswered questions: places where a person felt comfortable and sure of herself. As long as the keys remained mired in the portrait, Jamie knew she would be neither comfortable nor sure of herself in Miss Isabel's house.

"Oh, Jamie," Cade groaned, striding forward to pull her fiercely into his arms. "Don't look so shocked. You know damn well I wouldn't leave you alone in this house. I was only saying that to make you realize this situation requires some answers. And the only way we're going to get them is by taking a look at whatever is in that last letter from Fitzgerald."

The wave of unadulterated relief that washed over Jamie irritated her. She countered it by saying gruffly into his bare chest. "You're perfectly free to leave whenever you wish."

"Do you honestly think I'd leave without taking you with me? Tell me the truth, Jamie." He stroked her slender back and she quivered a little under the touch of his strong hand.

"No," she admitted on a sigh. "You're a very stubborn, determined, thorough man. You don't walk away from problems unless you've got another plan for solving them."

"You're right," he growled into her hair. "I see you did learn something about me, after all, during those two months in Santa Barbara. Something real."

"Yes. I learned something." It was the truth.

For a long moment they stood in silence. Jamie closed her eyes, her head on Cade's shoulder and tried to analyze her alternatives. They seemed very limited. The trap was almost closed. "Oh, Cade, I don't know what to do. I feel I should protect Miss Isabel's privacy—"

"There's one aspect of this situation you haven't considered," he interrupted quietly.

"What's that?"

"The risks involved might affect Miss Isabel."

Jamie lifted her head in surprise. "Miss Isabel! How could they affect her?"

Cade buried his hands in her tousled hair. "If someone was in this room last night looking for the letter or the safe-deposit-box key, that person didn't have to be Hadley Fitzgerald."

Shock went through Jamie as she absorbed the ramifications of his words. It was frightening enough to think of Hadley prowling around; the notion of a complete stranger in the house was terrifying. "I never thought of that."

"There are a lot of possibilities you haven't considered. Probably because your mind doesn't work along devious paths," he pointed out dryly.

"The way yours does, you mean?"

He winced. "The way mine does when the occasion requires," he temporized. "One problem we have to face is the possibility that someone else might be involved here. Someone very dangerous."

"But Hadley always worked alone!"

"The thing about big business is that it's never done in a vacuum. Someone else is always involved. It could be someone he fleeced. It could be a partner we don't know about. It could be anyone."

"We don't even know if there is someone prowling around," Jamie said desperately.

"Jamie, we know that whatever is in that package from Hadley, it was serious enough that Miss Isabel felt obliged to conceal it in a place of safekeeping. She didn't even confide in you and from what I've seen, that alone is cause for speculation."

"Yes," Jamie agreed wearily. "I didn't think she and I had any secrets from each other."

"She might have thought she was protecting you in some way by not letting you know what was in the package. But by concealing it, she might have been putting herself in danger."

"Perhaps. I don't know, Cade. I just don't know."

"Think about it, honey. In the morning we've got to act." Cade continued to run his fingers through her hair, his touch soothing and reassuring. "One way or another, we've got to do something."

He was right. Jamie knew he was right, but she didn't want to admit it. "In the morning," she repeated, buying herself a few more hours of time. "In the morning I'll decide what I'm going to do."

She felt him tighten and then relax as he accepted her words. "Then that leaves us with the rest of the night," he finally whispered. "I think we both could use some sleep."

Jamie realized she was being led back toward the bed. Belatedly she understood his intention. "Oh, no, Cade Santerre. You're not going to seduce me into doing what you want in the morning," she announced bluntly.

"You want to stay alone in this room tonight?" He smiled beguilingly down at her as he stopped beside the bed and began undoing the sash of her robe.

"Not particularly, but I also don't want you using any undue influence on me, either," she said tartly. "Cade, I mean it. I've got to have time to think. I want to consider my options." She put her hands over his, stopping him from unfastening the robe. Earnestly she looked up at him, willing him to understand.

"I know, sweetheart," he said seriously. "I know. I won't touch you. But I don't want to leave you alone, either."

"Where will you sleep?" she asked cautiously, glancing around the room.

"It's a big bed. I'll stay on my side. At least admit that you'll feel more comfortable with me in the room."

"What about you? Will you feel more comfortable staying here?" she countered wryly.

"It will be a very long night. But I've spent a lot of long nights during the past six weeks. I can handle another. Get into bed, honey. I'll check the locks and get the lights." He gave her a gentle push toward the bed and started across the room toward the door.

"Cade?"

He didn't look up from where he was examining the door lock. "What is it, honey?"

"Did you really spend a lot of long nights during the past six weeks?" She didn't know what made her ask and as soon as the words were out of her mouth she wished she hadn't spoken. The question shed far too much light on how she had spent her own nights during the past month and a half. Her pride protested violently.

"Lady, I spent more hours pacing the *Loophole*'s deck than I want to count." He shoved home the door's bolt with totally unnecessary force. Then he flipped the light switch.

Nestled in the shadows on her side of the bed, Jamie wondered if she was being naive and foolishly romantic to believe him.

Cade waited for Jamie's decision the next morning with the patience of a hunter. He knew he'd used the one lure Jamie would not be able to ignore. He had deliberately implied that the secret in the safe-deposit box might be a threat to Miss Isabel. The chance that her employer could be in potential jeopardy should give Jamie the final rationale she needed to unlock the bank box.

The thing was, he admitted to himself as he silently sipped coffee and munched peanut-butter toast, the lure wasn't exactly a fake. There was valid reason to suspect that the contents of Fitzgerald's letter were dangerous, both to Miss Isabel and to Jamie. Miss Isabel would not have taken such pains to hide the keys otherwise. He knew people and he knew motives. He'd had two months in the Fitzgerald household this summer, and he'd learned a lot about Miss Isabel. In spite of her flamboyantly artistic temperament, the older woman would not have hidden the keys in the painting unless she was very nervous about the contents of the safe-deposit box.

Cade was trying to manipulate Jamie again, and he knew it. But there was no other option this time. He had to protect her and that meant finding out the answer to the puzzle the keys represented. Damn it, none of the manipulation would be necessary if she would just trust him! Couldn't she see that he was only trying to take care of her?

Out of the corner of his eye Cade watched Jamie munch her own toast, her expression troubled and deeply thoughtful. Soon, he decided. She would let him know her decision very soon. She was on the brink. The minutes ticked past on the kitchen clock.

"All right," she finally said calmly, setting down her slice of toast. "If we can get the keys out of the painting, I'll take a look inside the safe-deposit box."

"Thank you, Jamie. It's for the best." Cade drew a

deep breath, trying to conceal his sense of relief. "You're doing this for Miss Isabel's sake as well as your own, you know."

"I have a feeling I'm doing this because you pushed me into it," she tossed back bluntly.

Cade looked at her. "I'm not forcing you to open the box."

"You dragged Miss Isabel's name into this so that I'd be able to tell myself I was still looking after her interests, didn't you?" She eyed him with speculation.

Briefly startled by her perception, Cade shook his head ruefully. "Maybe. But the reasoning holds. She could be in danger. She wouldn't have hidden those keys if she hadn't been worried about something, Jamie."

"I know."

"Jamie, I'm doing this for your own good."

She shot him a disgusted glance. "Don't you know that's just about the worst reason in the whole world to do something for anybody?"

Cade sighed. "Is it? I'm not used to deliberately doing things that are for someone else's good. Maybe I haven't handled it well."

Jamie grinned unexpectedly. "But you mean well, don't you, Cade? That's the only reason I'm doing this, you know. I've decided that although you are shrewd, manipulative and downright overbearing on occasion, I think you really do mean well this time."

"Your gratitude and praise are going to my head," he grumbled, reaching for his coffee.

"Well, don't let yourself feel too terribly giddy because I've got news for you. We're going to do this my way." Jamie took a certain satisfaction in the manner in which he received that bit of information.

"You want to run that by me again?" he asked coolly, watching her intently.

"Sure," she responded with a carelessness she was far from feeling. "We will not carry out this little project together. I will go into the safe-deposit box and I will take a look at the letter from Hadley. I will then tell you what I think you should know."

There was a rather menacing silence before Cade repeated far too softly, "You will tell me what you think I should know?"

She nodded once with just a hint of defiance. "I have been authorized to handle Miss Isabel's private affairs and make decisions regarding them. Furthermore, that safe-deposit box belongs to me, even though I never use it. Anyway you slice it, this is my job, Cade. Not yours. I did a lot of thinking about it last night and my decision is made. We do it my way or not at all."

Cade drew a deep breath before saying carefully, "Jamie, I think we had better discuss this."

She smiled brilliantly, feeling on top of the situation once more. "There is nothing to discuss."

"What would it take to make you trust me completely again?" he demanded with a harshness generated by frustration. "The way you trusted me this past summer? Just tell me, Jamie! Do I have to get down on my hands and knees and beg? Walk on coals? Sell my soul? Tell me what it will take, damn it!"

Jamie's brilliant smile faded. "We'd better get

started. It's a long drive into Carmel and we still have
to decide how to get the keys out of the painting."

Cade swore softly. "With a knife."

"I hate having to harm a piece of Miss Isabel's
work," Jamie said worriedly.

"I'll take the responsibility."

"It won't bother you at all, will it? Getting answers
is all that concerns you."

He threw her a savage glance as he got to his feet.
Then he strode around the kitchen counter and
yanked open a cutlery drawer. Selecting one of Miss
Isabel's finest knives, he headed for the bedroom without a word.

Belatedly Jamie scrambled off her stool and followed. She was involved in this, and regardless of
what Cade said about taking responsibility, there was
no way she could abdicate her own role in that respect.
She arrived in the bedroom doorway in time to see
Cade insert the knife into the painting as if he were filleting a fish. Jamie winced at the cool act of destruction. It was all over very quickly: neat and clean, if
somehow shocking. Hadley Fitzgerald continued to
gaze seriously out into the room, oblivious to the secrets that had just been exposed.

Silently Cade held up a small paint-encrusted plastic sandwich bag. The two keys were inside. Then he
headed down the hall, pausing impatiently while Jamie collected her oversize shoulder bag. As he walked
through the kitchen, Cade casually tossed the knife
onto the counter.

He remained silent until he had Jamie ensconced in

the Mazda and they were headed down the winding road toward Carmel. When he did speak his voice was cool and detached, almost clinical. A change had come over him since he'd freed the keys from the painting. He was very definitely all business.

"Since you won't let me look over your shoulder while you're going through the contents of that safe-deposit box, I want your promise to describe whatever it is as completely as possible. I need data, Jamie, if I'm ever going to figure this out. I must have a complete report on what you find. Do you understand?"

Uneasily Jamie nodded, realizing that he was right. "I understand."

"It would be a great relief to know that for a fact," he muttered.

Jamie said nothing in response, moodily watching the clouds that were gathering out at sea. There would be rain this afternoon, she thought distractedly.

In Carmel Cade parked the Mazda between a Mercedes and a Ferrari near the bank and escorted Jamie inside. At the gate to the safe-deposit vault he watched as she dutifully signed in and held out her key to the attendant. The bank clerk smiled and nodded and led her inside the steel-lined room. Nervously Jamie glanced back at Cade.

"Just be sure you look at every detail," he advised grimly.

Jamie nodded and quickly turned away. Inside the vault the clerk handed her the box and directed her to a private little cubicle.

"Ring the bell when you're finished. I'll put the box

away for you," the woman said cheerfully and closed the door.

Alone at last, Jamie thought ruefully and flipped open the lid of the box. She sat down at the single chair that had been provided and pulled out the letter from Hadley Fitzgerald. As she did so she disturbed a couple of small flat containers that were nestled deep inside the steel box. Curiously she reached out and picked one up, recognizing it by its shape. "Cade," she whispered to herself, "your famous instincts may be right. We may, indeed, have trouble."

For a long time Jamie sat staring at the small packages of recording tapes, wondering what Hadley had concealed on them. She read the letter to Miss Isabel a half-dozen times, and then she made up her mind. The trap she had sensed closing in around her seemed to shut just a little tighter. Instinct told her that soon there would be no room at all in which to maneuver. She would have to make a choice. Perhaps, she thought uneasily, she had made that choice when she had decided to contact Cade again. With a sigh Jamie removed the tapes and the letter, closed the box and rang for the attendant.

Cade waited with barely concealed impatience outside the little gate. When she came through he swung around quickly, his eyes going instantly to the letter and the tapes in her hand.

"Tapes?" he asked roughly.

Jamie nodded, not offering them to him. She dropped the packages of tapes into her oversize leather shoulder bag. "The letter doesn't say what's on them, only that Miss Isabel is to hide them."

"What's the date on the letter?" Cade demanded as he guided her out of the bank.

Jamie could feel the tension in him. The predator was very close to the prey, requiring enormous restraint for Cade not to simply pounce. She had seen the glittering anticipation in his eyes when she'd emerged from the cubicle with the contents of the safe-deposit box in her hand. No doubt he'd been very much afraid she would put them back in the vault.

"It's dated the twenty-first."

"The day before Hadley took the boat and disappeared," Cade muttered thoughtfully as he seated her in the Mazda. He closed the door and walked around the hood of the car to get in on the driver's side.

"The day you first made love to me," Jamie whispered to herself.

She watched him move lithely around the car and slide into the driver's seat. Apparently the personal significance of the date did not affect Cade one way or the other. He was busy sinking his teeth into the problem.

"So the letter by itself doesn't prove whether or not Fitzgerald's still alive." He expertly slid the Mazda out of the parking slot.

"No."

"We'll have to get a tape player so we can listen to what's on those tapes," he mused as he carefully negotiated the narrow Carmel street. It was Friday, and the weekend visitors were already arriving in droves to inundate the small village. Cars and pedestrians crowded the little streets. Behind the Mazda a plain dark Buick with heavily tinted windows struggled through the same throng.

"Miss Isabel has a machine," Jamie offered slowly. She fingered the strap of her bag as it lay in her lap, not at all certain about what to do next. "Though I'm not sure we have any right to listen to them, Cade."

"Jamie, the tapes are no different than the letter in that sense. Just another form of communication. We'll have to listen to them if we're going to figure out this mess."

"I suppose I could play them and then tell you if there's anything useful on them," she said slowly.

Cade's fingers tightened so severely on the wheel that his knuckles went white. But his voice was low and calm. "Yes," he agreed. "We can do it that way. It's a waste of time but we can do it. Given your lack of trust in me, I suppose it's the only alternative."

Jamie stared out the window, wondering if it was really pain she thought she heard in his words. She must make him understand that while her own trust in him was growing she was still torn by her sense of loyalty to her employer. Cade was beginning to demand that she make choices: choices that were dangerous and emotionally wrenching. "It's not a question of trust. Not exactly," she defended herself. "It's a matter of obligation to Miss Isabel. Can't you understand that, Cade?"

"It's a matter of trust," he countered bleakly. "Don't try to label it anything else."

The bitterness in his words lashed at her. *Oh, Cade,* Jamie thought, *you've got just about all I have to give. Do you need my complete and total loyalty, too?*

The clouds had grown heavy by the time Cade and Jamie reached the highway. Rain started before they had gone more than a couple of miles along the coastal road. The precipitation was driven by a sharp wind and drastically reduced visibility. Cade prudently slowed the Mazda and paid attention to his driving. He turned on the lights at about the same time the driver in the car behind turned on his. Cade glanced irritably into the rearview mirror.

"That's all I need in weather like this. A tailgater."

Automatically Jamie glanced back. The dark car was following rather close. "Probably scared to death on this road in this rain. Maybe he's using your taillights to navigate."

"Not a cheerful thought," Cade gritted.

Jamie slanted her companion an expressive glance. "You're in a lousy mood today, you know that?"

"I'm aware of it." Cade hit a fairly straight stretch of road and accelerated. The dark car picked up speed, too.

On the right the cliffs fell away to a wind-whipped surf. Jamie caught glimpses of the water foaming on the rocks as the rain swirled around the car. It was a spectacular sight, primeval and raw. Up ahead the short stretch of straight two-lane highway disappeared abruptly around a hairpin curve. Cade reluctantly began to ease off the accelerator.

"Son of a—" The rough, clipped oath was bitten off

savagely as Cade glanced once again into the rearview mirror. "The fool's going to try to pass!"

Startled at the act of folly, Jamie swung her head around in time to see the dark car maneuver out into the opposite lane and pick up speed with alarming suddenness. "You know, Cade, there's something familiar... Oh, my God!" Her breath caught as she realized what was about to happen.

"Cade, he's going to hit us!"

The warning came almost simultaneously with the impact. The dark car brushed the Mazda's side heavily and then seemed to bounce away. Cade was already reacting. He fought the dangerous curve and the protesting Mazda with a fierce grip on the wheel and ruthless footwork on the brakes and the accelerator.

The heavy dark car sideswiped the Mazda again, nearly sending it into the guardrail. Tires screeched and rubber burned as the battle for control of the little sports car was played out. The hairpin curve seemed to jackknife in front of Jamie's eyes, and for a timeless instant she was certain the next stop would be the bottom of the cliff. There was the violent sound of metal on metal as the Mazda scraped the rail.

Dimly aware that the dark car had surged ahead and was already out of sight around the sharp corner, Jamie dug her nails into the leather of her purse and wished she could squeeze shut her eyes. For some reason the small physical act seemed impossible. She was fated to watch the approaching doom through wide open eyes.

The world seemed to spin around her as Cade

hauled the Mazda back from the brink and forced it into a twisting turn. A few seconds later the car came to a halt with nerve-shattering abruptness. Jamie finally managed to blink. She found herself staring at the face of the mountain instead of the sea. The Mazda seemed to be tilted at a precarious angle, but at least it wasn't hanging over a sheer drop. Cade had swung it into the opposite lane and brought it to a stop against the rocky cliff. Jamie started to speak, swallowed and tried again.

"I have the oddest feeling this isn't going to do anything to improve your mood," she managed in an unnaturally thin voice.

"Full marks for your intuition," Cade growled. He flexed his hands on the steering wheel and looked at Jamie. His eyes moved quickly over her. "Are you all right?"

She nodded, wishing her pulse would slow. "Thanks to your driving. By any reasonable assessment of the situation we should be at the bottom of the cliff right now, trying to swim! My God, Cade, what on earth was that other driver thinking of?"

"An interesting question." Cade unlatched the door and pushed it open. "If I ever get my hands on him, I'll get an answer."

Jamie heard the ruthless fury in his cold words and shivered. "Where are you going, Cade?"

"We'll never get the car out of this ditch by ourselves. We'll have to walk. We're only a couple of miles from Miss Isabel's house. Get your jacket on, Jamie. The sooner we get started, the sooner we'll get there."

"I wish I'd brought an umbrella," Jamie groaned, trying to open her own door. It was impossible. The angle at which the car had come to rest prevented the door from opening more than a couple of inches.

"You'll have to get out on my side." Cade's hair was already soaked as he bent down to take her huge purse so that she could scramble out over the driver's seat.

Jamie handed the encumbering purse to him before she quite realized what she was doing. It was only as she saw his strong fingers close around the bag containing the tapes that it occurred to her it might be very difficult to regain possession.

"Uh, Cade...?"

"Hurry up, Jamie. I'm wet and I'm mad, and as you have already noted, I am not in the best of moods. This isn't a good time to bring up the subject of trust, loyalty and obligation. You'll get your damn purse back as soon as you get out of the car. You think I want to hike two miles carrying this forty-pound sucker?"

"Probably not," she agreed as she found her footing in the mud. "I...I wasn't accusing you of trying to take it," she began uncertainly.

"Jamie, right now, the less said, the better. For both of us."

It was a long, wet and thoroughly miserable walk. The rain made Jamie's glasses more of a hindrance than a help. She removed them and stuck them into her purse. There were several points along the way when Jamie wished devoutly that it was Cade and not herself carting the heavy shoulder bag, but she could hardly ask for help after that little scene at the car. By the time they reached the driveway of Miss Isabel's house, she felt as though the purse really did weigh forty pounds.

"I've been hallucinating about a hot shower and a warm brandy for the past half hour," Jamie said as she slogged toward the front door, head down against the driving rain.

"You're going to have to go on dreaming a while longer," Cade declared softly as he came to an unexpected halt. His hands closed over Jamie's shoulder, bringing her to a stop.

Annoyed, Jamie squinted up at him through the pouring rain. "What on earth are you talking about?"

"We've got company."

Jamie turned her head, able to perceive that there were lights on inside the house. She knew she had turned them off before leaving earlier in the day. "Good heavens! Who in the world could be inside? Burglars?"

"I'm not sure, but I have a hunch it's not your ordinary, run-of-the-mill burglar. Not today and not with the way my luck has been running lately."

"You and your instincts," Jamie muttered, trying to peer through the rain-dark afternoon. She reached inside her purse for her glasses and succeeded in shoving them onto her nose just as the front door opened. The sight of the familiar silver-haired figure standing on the threshold sent a jolt of alarm along Jamie's senses.

"Miss Isabel!" she gasped.

NINE

"Jamie, wait!" Cade caught hold of her shoulder just as Jamie lifted her arm to wave to Miss Isabel. "Listen to me before you dash over there."

The harsh urgency in his words stopped Jamie in her tracks. Through rain-streaked lenses she stared at him, waiting impatiently for whatever it was he felt obliged to say. Miss Isabel stood several yards away, sheltered in the doorway.

"What is it now, Cade? Can't it wait until we're in the house? I'm soaked to the skin, and I can't wait to ask Miss Isabel what happened to bring her home early from the cruise. Maybe she discovered something important about Hadley. Or maybe she got ill."

He held her full attention with the cold hard gold in his eyes. Cade's face was set in steel, and the strong hand on her shoulder conveyed the overwhelming volume of his will. "Jamie, I'm going to ask something of you. Something crucial. It's for your sake as well as mine, although I don't expect you'll believe me."

"Cade, I'm not in the mood for heavy drama. What are you trying to say?"

"I want you to promise me you won't tell Miss Isabel you've got those tapes in your purse. Let me handle that part of the story."

"But, Cade, that's ridiculous! Why shouldn't I tell her? They belong to her. After all, they're from her brother."

"I'm not going to steal them from her, I'm just trying to buy some time!"

"Time for what?" Jamie flared, moving uneasily under the hard pressure of his hand. She sensed the determination in him, and knew he was deadly serious.

"Time to figure out what in hell is going on," he snapped. "Jamie, that car that sideswiped us back there on the highway..."

"What about it?" she asked, frowning.

"I think the timing of that accident was rather coincidental. It didn't take place until after we had those tapes in our possession."

"Cade, that's absurd." But her eyes narrowed as she took in the full implications of his words. She remembered thinking just before the accident that there had been something familiar about the plain dark Buick. Was it the car she had seen at the gas station, she wondered. The one that had been driven by the man who resembled Hadley Fitzgerald?

"I also think that whatever is on those tapes is dangerous. If it weren't, Fitzgerald wouldn't have asked Miss Isabel to hide them. Jamie, I haven't got time to convince you logically of what I'm saying. All I can tell you is that every instinct I've got is screaming. I'm going to have to ask you to trust me. I know that's demanding a lot under the circumstances—"

"Yes, it is, Cade," she interrupted coolly.

His mouth tightened. "Damn it, woman, I love you and I think that once you're through punishing both of us for what happened this summer, you'll realize you love me. That relationship gives me the right to make a few demands, especially when your life may be at stake!"

Jamie's mouth fell open. She closed it immediately when she tasted rain. Behind the lenses of her glasses her eyes widened in astonishment. "You love me?" she squeaked. Her brain ignored the rest of his statement, focusing entirely on the first few words. She couldn't believe he'd said them. "You love me," she whispered wonderingly.

He looked down at her rain-drenched face. "Why in hell do you think I agreed to get involved with Miss Isabel's screwy hunt for her brother? Why would I be putting up with your temperamental moods and your notions of revenge if I didn't love you? For God's sake, Jamie, this isn't the time to discuss that subject in detail, either. You're going to have to trust me."

Vividly aware of Miss Isabel waiting in the doorway, Jamie knew she couldn't stand around in the rain asking for explanations and protestations of love. There would be time for that later. Cade was right. At the moment she had to make a decision. She gripped the leather bag more fiercely as she tried to search his rain-streaked face for the truth.

"I'll...I'll agree to follow your lead until I decide for certain what's going on," she temporized.

Cade wanted to shake her. Couldn't she see the danger they were in? There was no time to go over all the details for her benefit. No time to add up the various and sundry little things that went together to form an alarming pattern. He was going on instinct and a view of the world that was far more cynical than Jamie's. After his investigations this summer he knew for a fact just how deeply involved in criminal activity Hadley Fitzgerald had been. Whatever was on those tapes had to be incriminating and therefore dangerous.

Jamie, however, functioned under an entirely different view of the universe, one that inclined toward the benefit of the doubt until proven otherwise. As far as she was concerned, Cade had given up his right to that benefit of a doubt by his actions this summer. Miss Isabel, on the other hand, had two full years of friendship going for her. She had done nothing to crush Jamie's belief in her integrity the way Cade knew he had.

Cade felt a devastating wave of helplessness. It was too late to try to reason with Jamie. He could only hope that her underlying feelings for him would surface in this moment of crisis. On top of that hope, he was counting on love being a stronger bond than the loyalty she felt toward Miss Isabel.

Cade was all too well aware that he was pinning a great deal on a very insubstantial and unproven foundation. He had, after all, no proof that Jamie loved him. On top of that he had ample proof that she distrusted him. The fact that her life might depend on the outcome of her decision only served to infuriate him because it reinforced his sense of helplessness.

"Jamie, please trust me," he heard himself say, but he didn't know if she heard him. She was already turning away and starting toward the house. Unable to do anything else, Cade followed.

"Miss Isabel! What on earth are you doing here? Why aren't you in Samoa? What happened?" Jamie's questions bubbled over as she hurried to get under the shelter of the eaves. "Watch out," she added quickly as Miss Isabel started to hug her, "I'm soaking wet!"

"So I see. And Cade is also. Whatever made you two decide to take a walk in this weather?" Miss Isabel stepped back into the hall and held the door.

"It's a long story," Cade began calmly as he bent down to remove his mud-splattered shoes. "And before we start explanations, I think Jamie and I had better have a shower and get into some warm clothes."

"Yes, of course," Miss Isabel agreed instantly. "Run along, both of you, and I'll fix some hot tea."

"But, Miss Isabel, what happened?" Jamie asked as Cade took her arm and started her down the hall to the bedrooms.

Miss Isabel smiled, her eyes animated. "Mine is a long story, too, dear. Suffice it to say that I've found Hadley. Or perhaps I should say he found me."

"Hadley!" Jamie gasped. "He's alive?"

"I told you I had a feeling he was," Miss Isabel said. "Now hurry up with that shower. I'll see you in the kitchen."

Jamie lifted a perplexed face to Cade as he strode down the hall with her in tow. "Cade, she says he's alive!"

"I heard."

"What in the world is going on?" Jamie wondered aloud, feeling dazed by the turn of events.

"Let me have the tapes, Jamie," Cade ordered softly as he pushed open the door to the bedroom he had been using.

"Why? What are you going to do with them?"

"Nothing brilliantly clever, unfortunately. I just thought I'd try to make them a little more inaccessible than they are at the moment." His eyes never leaving hers, Cade shut the bedroom door and reached for the leather bag.

For a wary moment Jamie hesitated. Then slowly, reluctantly she released the purse. Without a word Cade unzipped it, removed the packages of tapes and dumped them into the big cloisonné jar.

"What good will that do?" Jamie asked bewilderedly.

"You never know. Sometimes it pays to have something with which to bargain," Cade said cryptically. He gave her a level glance. "Of course, bargaining doesn't do much good if one party insists on giving away the objects with which one is negotiating. You might keep that in mind later, Jamie."

"I don't understand what you're talking about," she protested.

"You will soon enough," he said, sighing. "Get into the shower, Jamie."

"My clothes..."

"I'll dig some out and leave them in the dressing room."

"What about you? You need a shower, too," she pointed out gently.

"I'll skip the shower and use a towel." His mouth crooked wryly. "What's the matter? Afraid I was going to insist on sharing? You don't have to worry about that today. I've got other things on my mind." He peeled off his wet shirt.

Jamie eyed him for a moment, and then the light dawned. "You're going to stand guard out here, aren't you?"

"Let's just say I don't think this is a good time for both of us to be playing water games."

"Cade, you can't possibly believe Miss Isabel is plotting to...to harm us!"

"Jamie, I don't know what to believe," Cade said wearily. "I only know we've got to take a few precautions until we get this mess sorted out. Now go take your shower."

She turned to obey and then paused once more to ask tremulously, "Cade, did you mean what you said out there? Do you really love me?"

"I love you, Jamie."

Jamie's heart sang with hope. "Oh, Cade, when did you first realize it? This past summer or during those six weeks we were apart?" An instant later she knew her eagerness was a mistake.

"For crying out loud, Jamie, we've got a serious situation on our hands in case you haven't noticed,"

Cade snapped. "This is hardly the time for that sort of discussion!"

Jamie bit her lip. "You don't sound like a man in love."

"Go take your shower." Cade turned away and began to unzip the wet jeans he was wearing. His tension was plain in the taut lines of his bare shoulders.

Jamie stepped into the bathroom and closed the door behind her, wondering at her curious sense of hovering again on the edge of a precipice. It was the unknowns that plagued her, she thought as she stepped under the hot shower. For a few moments she had truly believed Cade loved her. Now she was not so sure. He was very intent on gaining her cooperation at the moment. He was a very perceptive man in some respects and he might have realized that the surest way of gaining her allegiance was to claim he loved her. If he had come to realize that she loved him, he would know what a powerful tool he held. *Please*, she thought desperately, *please Cade, don't use my love to try and control me. I can handle anything else, but not that.*

Out in the other room Cade finished drying himself, pulled on fresh clothes and paced the floor, questioning his approach to the problem he faced. He had been a fool to let those six weeks go by without contacting Jamie. He realized that now. At the time it had seemed the best way to handle her. But those six weeks had apparently given her plenty of opportunity to question him and his motives, rather than to make her long for him.

Bad timing and bad planning. Cade was disgusted

with himself. But everything had been like that around Jamie. Nothing seemed to go right. Now he was trapped, forced to rely on her very weak trust in him.

While Miss Isabel seemed to enjoy unlimited loyalty from Jamie.

He whirled too abruptly when Jamie emerged from the bathroom, dressed in the jeans and red knit top he had selected for her. Instantly he realized that his quick movement came across as somehow menacing. Cade swore silently and forced himself to exert the full measure of his self-control.

"Ready? Remember, I'm not saying that Miss Isabel is a criminal..."

"I should hope not!"

"All I'm asking," Cade continued doggedly, "is that you let me take the lead. Let me be the one to give her information. Just back me up, okay?"

Jamie nodded unwillingly, wishing desperately that she could read his mind. Then she started toward the door.

Miss Isabel was waiting in the kitchen, busying herself with the teakettle. She looked up as Jamie and Cade walked into the warm, cozy room. "Ah, there you are. You look much better now. Not like a couple of drowned rats. Here, have some tea." She poured into the two cups she had set out. The atmosphere in the room was charming and gracious. Jamie began to relax. Cade's sense of urgency had really begun to affect her, she realized.

"Tell us what happened, Miss Isabel," Jamie said,

sliding onto a stool beside Cade. The knife Cade had used earlier to pry the keys out of the painting was still lying on the counter where he had tossed it. Jamie swallowed a guilty feeling as she saw the flecks of paint on the blade. She wondered if Miss Isabel had noticed the damaged painting in the bedroom. Apparently not, or probably she would have already said something about it. "How did Hadley find you?"

"He was waiting in Tahiti. Met me at the ship when we docked. I was never so astounded in my entire life!"

"How did he know where to find you?"

"Oh, that was simple enough. He contacted his lawyer a week ago and found out from him that I had left on the cruise a week earlier. It wasn't hard to get the ship's itinerary." Miss Isabel poured herself a cup of tea.

"Where is he now?" Cade asked calmly.

"Still out of the country. He doesn't dare come back until he can prove his innocence." Miss Isabel turned bright, excited eyes on Jamie. "Remember that package that was waiting for me when we got back from Santa Barbara?"

Jamie swallowed as more guilt assailed her. "Yes," she managed in a reasonably steady voice. Beside her she felt Cade's increasing tension.

"Well, that package contains the proof of Hadley's innocence," Miss Isabel declared triumphantly. She went on in a rush. "We have to get it out of the bank vault and play the tapes for that Mr. Gallagher person. Hadley says everything will be all right once Gal-

lagher understands who was really behind the land-
fraud deals. Hadley was just a pawn. He didn't realize
what was going on behind the scenes, you see. He had
simply agreed to broker the deals. Naturally he assumed things were legitimate. But the people who had
set it all up let him take the blame when things went
wrong. Hadley was forced to run."

"I see," Jamie said slowly, trying to think. Now was
the time. She had to tell Miss Isabel she already had
the tapes. Jamie realized the only thing that was pre-
venting her from blurting out the full truth was Cade's
silent command. She could feel him willing her not to
say the words, and for the life of her, Jamie found herself keeping her mouth shut.

"Miss Isabel," Cade began quietly, "I think you
should know that Jamie and I have already been to the
bank."

Miss Isabel looked startled. "But the keys..."

"We found the keys in the painting. I convinced Jamie that it was necessary to see what was in the package from your brother."

Miss Isabel turned apologetic eyes on Jamie. "Forgive me for hiding your keys, my dear. At the time I
thought it was for the best. I had no idea what was in
that package, you see, and I wanted to protect you."

Jamie exhaled on a sigh of relief and gratitude. Cade
had decided not to lie to Miss Isabel. She started to
smile reassuringly at her employer, but the expression
faded as Cade went on coolly.

"We picked up the tapes, but as yet we haven't
played them."

"Where are they?" Miss Isabel demanded, some of her gracious manner fading as she turned to gaze intently at Cade.

"In a safe place," Cade told her neutrally.

"I don't understand." The older woman's brow furrowed.

"I hid them," Cade said simply. "You see there was an accident on the way back from the bank this afternoon."

"An accident!" Miss Isabel looked thunderstruck. "Is that why you two were walking? Something happened to your car?"

"We were sideswiped by another car," Jamie put in quickly. "Almost sent us off the road into the ocean. Fortunately Cade managed to hold things together. We ended up in a ditch instead of the sea."

"Good heavens!"

"It was a little grim for a few minutes," Cade said dryly. "And afterward I was left wondering if the incident hadn't been deliberate. As Jamie can tell you, I tend to take a rather cynical view of life."

"But who would do such a thing deliberately?" Miss Isabel asked.

"Someone who wanted the tapes." Cade let the words hang in the air for a moment before adding smoothly, "Perhaps the people your brother claims framed him."

Jamie's head came around, her eyes as startled as Miss Isabel's. "Cade, do you really think...?"

"I don't know what to think at this point," Cade said patiently, his eyes on Miss Isabel. "I'm trying to put all the pieces of the puzzle together but I'm still missing a few answers."

Some of the animation left Miss Isabel's face. "Where did you hide the tapes?"

"I stuffed them into a plastic sack and left them under a rock about halfway between here and the spot where the Mazda got shoved off the road," Cade said quite casually. "If that accident had been deliberate, the wrong people might have been waiting for us here, you see. I didn't want to take any chances." He didn't even glance at Jamie, who went very still as she listened to the outright lie.

"Oh, my God," Miss Isabel whispered, looking stricken. "We've got to get them!"

"They'll be safe," Cade soothed. "The plastic bag will protect them from the moisture."

"No, you don't understand," Miss Isabel said agitatedly.

Jamie couldn't abide her employer's obvious distress. "Miss Isabel, stop worrying. The tapes are safe, believe me. You said your brother wants them played for Gallagher and his team. Well, we'll do exactly that. We'll get them and take them down to L.A. and play them for Gallagher. Won't we, Cade?" she added deliberately.

Cade shrugged easily. "Sounds like a logical plan to me."

Miss Isabel shook her head quickly. "Hadley wants me to get them and take them to him. He wants to be the one to go to Gallagher. Don't you see? That way there won't be any question of his innocence. He can interpret them properly to the authorities. If someone else is after those tapes we've got to move quickly. It would be terrible if the others discovered them first!"

"No one will find them, Miss Isabel," Cade told her.

She studied his calm, controlled face for a long moment and then appeared to reach a decision. She turned to Jamie.

"Jamie, dear, I'm afraid I must insist that you fetch the tapes," Miss Isabel ordered very softly. "We can go and get them together."

"No," Cade interrupted quietly. "Jamie's not going to get the tapes for you."

Jamie tensed, sensing that the trap in which she had found herself was finally about to close completely. She knew she was going to be forced to choose between her duty to Miss Isabel and her trust in Cade.

"Miss Isabel, Cade thinks it would be dangerous for you to have the tapes. If someone is out to get them then whoever has them is in jeopardy," Jamie argued desperately, seeking a way to resolve the dilemma without being forced to hurt Miss Isabel.

"You must trust me to know what's best, Jamie," Miss Isabel told her gently. "I'm the one who's seen Hadley. I know how he wants this matter handled. Now go get your rain coat, dear. We must hurry."

Jamie turned appealing eyes on Cade, but there was no help from that quarter. "Everyone around here seems to be acting in my best interests," she observed dryly.

"Don't move, Jamie. The tapes are safe enough for the moment, and I don't want you near them."

Miss Isabel frowned. "Jamie, I really must insist. You are, after all, my employee, and I'm afraid that if necessary I'll have to make this request an order. Please don't forget that the tapes are rightfully mine."

"I know, Miss Isabel, but if they're dangerous—"

"They're dangerous," Cade interrupted coldly. "Believe me. If you turn them over to Miss Isabel, all of us will be in danger."

"Cade!"

"What are you talking about, Cade?" Miss Isabel demanded.

"Just that right now the location of the tapes is the only bargaining point Jamie and I've got. I intend to hang on to it for both our sakes. I'm not going to let her risk her neck by turning them over to you."

"Risk my neck!" Jamie exclaimed. "What *are* you talking about, Cade? You said it was Miss Isabel you were trying to protect."

"I'm trying to protect all of us, but I'm not getting a hell of a lot of cooperation." Cade reached out and caught hold of her chin, forcing her to face him. Tawny eyes burned down into her anxious gaze. "I mean it, Jamie. If you care about what happens to yourself, to me or even to Miss Isabel, you will do as I say."

She had to make a choice. In that moment Jamie hated both Miss Isabel and Cade for forcing her into the painful decision. She had seen this moment bearing down on her for a long while, and now that it was here she was strangely furious. She had striven to avoid having to take this risk, but she should have known that there was no way around it. For a timeless moment she studied Cade's implacable gaze, and then she turned wearily to her employer. The reason she had always feared finding herself up against the wall was because deep down she had known what her choice would be. The trap had closed. She loved Cade, and now she had to trust him. Completely. She was being forced to make a final statement about her loyalties and her priorities. Faced with no other alternative, Jamie made the only choice she could. She had to back her lover.

"I'm sorry, Miss Isabel, but I think Cade is right. The tapes are dangerous, and we'd better let him handle them. He'll know what to do with them." Beside her she felt Cade inhale deeply, as though he had just finished a long race. She was vaguely astounded that he had been so tense about her decision.

"This is ridiculous!" Miss Isabel bit out. "Jamie, you can't do this. You work for me! We're friends. You have to do as I say."

"You're quite right," declared a cultivated male voice from behind Jamie. "This is ridiculous. I told you your way wasn't going to work, Isabel. I know Cade Santerre too well. I think it's time we put a stop to this silly game. Foolish of me to let you try your approach first, Isabel. It's obvious that Mr. Santerre has already been put on alert. And once Mr. Santerre has the scent, he never lets up until he's bagged his quarry. Isn't that correct, Cade?"

"I do my best to finish things, Fitzgerald," Cade said calmly. Of all the people in the room, he seemed the least surprised to see Hadley.

Jamie swung around on the stool, staring at Hadley Fitzgerald. The polished, cultured appearance of Miss Isabel's charming brother was rather marred by the gun he held in one hand. He was gripping the weapon very tightly, as if he were not at ease with it. She watched him, frozen in astonishment, and wondered inanely why she had never noticed the lack of warmth in Hadley's eyes. Good manners could certainly cover a multitude of secrets, she realized, feeling dazed.

"I thought you were waiting somewhere outside the country for the tapes." Jamie felt stupid and shaken. She decided then and there that Cade's concerns had been valid, to say the least.

"And instead he was waiting in the pantry. He couldn't risk turning this little job over to his sister, could you, Fitzgerald?" Cade swiveled slowly on the stool so that he was facing Hadley and the gun. His eyes went briefly to the overly fierce grip Fitzgerald was applying to the weapon. With an absent movement Cade rested his arm on the counter, his hand near the kitchen knife. "Too much is riding on getting back those tapes. What exactly is on them, anyway? Details of how you worked other scams? Blackmail information? Conversations with people who didn't know they were being recorded and who would probably react violently if they found out?"

"Proof of his innocence is on those tapes!" Miss Isabel cried.

Hadley nodded pleasantly. "Exactly. So I'm afraid I really must ask you to fetch them, Jamie. I find I don't want to spend the rest of my life living outside the country. So inconvenient. So few places like Santa Barbara. Once I play those tapes for Gallagher and explain the entire situation, I'll be free to return."

Cade said nothing, his derisive disbelief clear in his seemingly relaxed pose.

Jamie licked her lower lip. "Are you really going to play the tapes for Gallagher?"

"Just as soon as I get my hands on them," Hadley Fitzgerald declared vehemently. "Isabel told me she had put them in your safe-deposit box, and that either you or she had access. I slipped back into the country a couple of days ago. Isabel flew in late yesterday. After all, it wouldn't have done me any good just to get my hands on the keys. I needed Isabel to open the safe-deposit box. When she told me Santerre was probably starting to search for me, I knew there would be trouble. And I was right, wasn't I, Santerre? You'll do anything to see me in jail. You're never going to accept the fact that your sister and her husband got into financial trouble out of sheer stupidity, not because I victimized them. You were out for revenge this summer, not justice. So you came looking for me. You managed to plant enough false evidence around my home to convince Gallagher that I was guilty of fraud."

Jamie moved restlessly and glanced at Miss Isabel. The older woman looked distraught.

"If only I'd known, Jamie," she said sadly. "I would never have allowed you to talk me into hiring Cade to find Hadley."

"It was Jamie's idea to hire me?" Cade sounded

only mildly interested, but Jamie sensed his acute attention.

"Yes. She said you were a very thorough man, and that by the end of the summer you probably knew more about Hadley's way of doing things than anyone else on earth, even me. And I suppose she was right." Miss Isabel sighed. "She and I both made the mistake of thinking you were only doing a job when you went after poor Hadley the first time. Now I know you were out for revenge because you thought he had defrauded your sister. You must have been very angry when my brother slipped through your fingers. When Jamie showed up offering you the task of finding out whether or not he was still alive, you couldn't resist having another go at him, could you?"

"Your brother did defraud my sister and a lot of others, as well," Cade said flatly. "If he weren't guilty as hell why would he be holding a gun on me now?"

"Because I know there's no other way to get those tapes back from you," Hadley put in. "Jamie, my dear, you've been used. Santerre has used you from the first."

"Yes, Jamie," Miss Isabel said quickly. "It's the truth. You must realize that by now. The fact that he won't turn the tapes over to their rightful owner is proof enough. Surely this time around you can see him for what he is."

Jamie didn't look at Cade as she answered the other woman. "Yes, Miss Isabel, I can see him for what he is. He's the man I love. And that doesn't leave me much choice. I have to trust him."

"Jamie, no!" Isabel pleaded.

"Not a smart move, Jamie." But Hadley didn't appear surprised by her words. He seemed to have expected something like that.

"Perhaps not," Cade agreed sardonically, his eyes on Jamie. "But for better or worse she's made her decision. And that leaves you with a problem, Fitzgerald."

"The same problem I've had all along. I need those tapes."

"I know. So why don't we get down to business?"

Not understanding, Jamie snapped her head around to stare at Cade. "What business?"

Cade wasn't looking at her now. His whole attention was on Hadley. "The business of trading those tapes for our lives."

Jamie's breath seemed to falter, and Miss Isabel bit back a small scream as she glanced at her brother and then at Cade.

"Your lives!" Isabel managed in tones of shock. "No, no, you don't understand..."

"I'm very much afraid he does, Isabel." Hadley smiled genially. "We appear to have arrived at the bargaining point."

"You're going to kill us?" Jamie could feel the fear crawling unpleasantly through her stomach. She hoped she wouldn't be sick all over the kitchen floor. "For those tapes?"

"No, no, my dear," Hadley corrected her. "I'm only going to kill you if your lover doesn't turn the tapes over to me. But I'm sure Mr. Santerre will be reasonable about this, won't you, Cade?"

Cade inclined his head politely. "Very reasonable."

"Where are the tapes?"

"In a safe place."

"Please, Cade," Miss Isabel interjected, wringing her hands, "tell him where they are."

"If I do that, Isabel, Jamie and I won't leave here alive. We need to work out the terms of the trade, don't we Hadley? You need the tapes, and Jamie and I want to live. Just out of curiosity, what will you do once you have your hands on those recordings?"

"Leave the country again. I plan to invest in some land-development projects down in the Caribbean. I'll keep myself amused there for a few years until everyone here in the States has forgotten about me. People always forget about this sort of thing in time."

"But if you plan to stay out of the country, why did you risk coming back for the tapes?" Jamie asked.

"I'm afraid one of Mr. Santerre's guesses a few minutes ago was accurate. There are conversations on those tapes. Conversations with people who would be most incensed if they knew they had been recorded. If those tapes were ever played for Gallagher or someone like him, they would lead to all sorts of interesting investigations. And they would probably get me killed. The people whose voices are on those tapes would likely go to jail, and they wouldn't care for that. They have the power and the, shall we say, inclination to punish people responsible for causing them that sort of inconvenience. Regardless of where I was living, they'd find me. They were, I'm afraid, less than respectable business associates of mine who occasionally backed some of my projects."

"Why did you record them?" Jamie struggled to put it all together.

"At the time it probably seemed like an insurance policy, didn't it, Fitzgerald?" Cade supplied the answer easily. "You thought that if your business partners ever turned threatening or nasty, you'd have the tapes. You could have used them as blackmail or to trade with someone like Gallagher for protective custody."

Hadley nodded easily. "As you say, at the time it seemed like a good idea. But I started getting nervous about you in Santa Barbara, Santerre. So I thought I'd take a few protective measures and drop the tapes in the mail to Isabel along with instructions to hide them until I could collect them. I didn't want them in the house. Unfortunately, I didn't know just how dangerous the situation was. The day after I mailed them I realized everything was going to collapse much sooner than I had expected. I got a warning from a business acquaintance who had received word that Mr. Gallagher knew Mr. Santerre. More of a coincidence than I cared to contemplate. I decided to leave everything and run. I thought the fake suicide was a nice touch. I hired a certain person whom I had occasionally used for other purposes to take the boat out to sea and abandon it."

"While you left the country under another name?" Cade concluded.

"Exactly. You're very astute, Santerre. A most perceptive man."

"I try," Cade said dryly. "Sometimes I'm a little slow on the uptake, but I try."

"You should have tried a little harder. Now you're in a rather awkward situation, aren't you?"

"I know where the tapes are, and I'm willing to deal," Cade reminded him.

"How do you propose we go about this little trade?"

"You and I will go together to get the tapes. Jamie leaves here in the meantime and heads for a motel where she will wait until I contact her."

Jamie panicked. "No, I won't leave you behind with him!"

"You will do as I say, Jamie," Cade told her icily.

"On the contrary," Fitzgerald said. "You will both do as I say. And I'm not sure your plan provides me with adequate protection, Santerre. Jamie could go to the cops instead of a motel."

"She won't. Not if she knows my life would be forfeit." Cade sounded absolutely certain of that.

Miss Isabel interrupted in painful tones. "Please, Hadley. Is all this necessary?"

"I'm afraid so, Isabel."

Isabel turned unhappy eyes on Jamie. "Jamie, dear, I'm so sorry it had to be like this. Please believe me, I never meant you any harm. It's just that when Hadley explained to me what serious jeopardy he was in because of what was on those tapes, I knew I didn't have any choice but to get them back for him. Surely you can understand?"

Jamie looked at her and then said slowly, "I understand, Miss Isabel. We all have our own priorities when it comes to giving our loyalty and trust to another human being, don't we?" She thought she saw tears in Miss Isabel's eyes, and she wanted to put her arms around the older woman and offer comfort. But that was impossible. Isabel stood on the other side of the invisible line of loyalty that had been drawn down the middle of the kitchen. Everyone in the room had made his or her own choice, and now there was no going back.

Hadley Fitzgerald eyed Jamie with a shrewd gaze and came to a decision. "All right, Santerre, I'm inclined to believe your analysis of the situation is correct. You always seemed to have a knack for knowing what motivates people, and I think you're right about Jamie. She's in love with you, and she won't do anything to put you in greater danger than you already are. I'll go along with your plan with one modification."

"What's that?"

"My sister accompanies Jamie to the motel just to make certain there are no last minute complications."

Cade thought about that. "All right," he agreed. "When do we leave?"

"Immediately. I don't wish to stay in the country any longer than absolutely necessary. Run along and get your things, Jamie. Isabel, go with her."

Wordlessly Jamie looked at Cade, willing him to

change his mind. She felt panicked: no longer trusting either Hadley or Miss Isabel, and very much afraid that there was far more risk involved for Cade than he seemed to acknowledge. The last thing she wanted to do was leave Cade alone with Hadley and the gun.

"Do as he says," Cade said gently. "Run along and get your purse and keys. Then take Isabel's Audi and drive to San Francisco."

"How will you contact me later?" she asked desperately.

"Phone the marina and leave a return phone number. I'll call there and get the message. Then I'll call you."

"Cade, I don't think this is a good idea," she said urgently.

"Get going, Jamie," he commanded softly. "Just get the hell out of here, will you?"

Jamie knew he meant it. Swallowing the rest of her protests, she spun around and started down the hall to her bedroom. After an anxious glance at her brother, Miss Isabel quickly followed.

Something wasn't right about the trade that had been arranged, Jamie thought distractedly as she opened the door to the bedroom. Hadley had agreed to it too readily, for one thing.

"I'm so sorry, Jamie. You can't imagine how upset I am about all this," Isabel said unhappily as she watched Jamie cross the room to pick up the oversize purse. "But there really is no choice. I must help protect Hadley. He's my brother."

"I understand, Miss Isabel."

"And he's explained to me just how vengeful and relentless Cade can be. Hadley says he's like a lion on the hunt. He's clever and ruthless. He'll do anything to bring down his prey."

"Hadley may be right," Jamie began wryly and then realized what she was saying. Hadley *was* right! And Fitzgerald was shrewd enough to know what to expect from his enemy if he turned him loose. No place on earth would be safe for Hadley Fitzgerald after this confrontation. Cade would track him down and make him pay for having put Jamie in such danger. It was probably Hadley who had tried to force the Mazda off the road this afternoon, Jamie realized. Then he'd threatened her with a gun.

Cade would be cold-bloodedly furious. He would also be relentless about bringing Hadley to justice. Failing that, he would deal out his own justice.

Jamie knew it and so did Hadley Fitzgerald, she was certain. Fitzgerald could simply not afford to let Cade live. If she meekly left the house with Miss Isabel, she would be leaving Cade alone with a man who fully intended to kill him. She would be abandoning the man she loved to his executioner.

TEN

"Miss Isabel, I can't leave here with you." Jamie turned at the window, the heavy shoulder bag in her hand. She looked straight into the older woman's eyes. "Hadley will kill Cade."

Miss Isabel stared back, her face crumpling. When she spoke there was a new, almost hysterical harshness in her voice. "I'm afraid you have no choice, Jamie." She reached into her pocket and withdrew a tiny but lethal looking handgun. Her fingers trembled, and she held the weapon as though she hated it, but she pointed it straight at Jamie. "And I don't have any choice, either. I must help Hadley. You and I will leave here while Cade shows Hadley where the tapes are. You must, Jamie. It's the only way. I must help Hadley! He's my brother."

"Miss Isabel!" Dumbfounded by the appearance of the gun in Isabel's talented fingers, Jamie could barely speak.

"I'm sorry, Jamie. Please believe me. I'm very, very sorry."

"So am I." Jamie's next action was not premeditated. She only knew that she had to do something. Miss Isabel held a gun, and that gun would provide the edge Jamie needed to help Cade. In that moment nothing seemed as important as taking the weapon from Miss Isabel.

She flung out her hand, sending the heavy purse straight into the huge cloisonné jar that held the tapes. The elegant vase toppled and crashed to the floor. The carpet was not sufficient padding to protect it. The jar broke into a hundred pieces with a shattering sound, and the tapes tumbled free.

Miss Isabel shrieked, whether at the destruction of the beautiful object she had created or at the sight of the tapes, Jamie never knew. As Isabel whirled to stare in shock at the shattered vase, Jamie leaped forward.

There was an enraged scream of pain from the kitchen just as Jamie grabbed Isabel's arm. It sent a jolt of terror through Jamie until she realized it was Hadley's and not Cade's voice she had heard. Frantically she grabbed at the gun in her employer's hand.

It was a simple matter to wrench the small weapon from Miss Isabel's fingers. The older woman didn't even seem to notice. She was mesmerized by the sight of the destroyed vase.

Holding the gun uncertainly—she had never held one before in her life—Jamie took a last look at Isabel and decided there was no danger from that quarter. Desperately she spun around and flung open the door.

"Jamie!" Cade's voice came from the kitchen, fierce and demanding.

"I'm okay, Cade! What's going on?"

"It's all right, Jamie," he shouted from the kitchen. "Get in here where I can see you. I don't trust Isabel."

Jamie ran down the hall, halting abruptly in the kitchen doorway to stare at Hadley's sprawled form. He was lying on the floor, clutching his arm in obvious agony. The kitchen knife that had been sitting on the counter was sticking out of his shoulder. Dazedly Jamie lifted her eyes to Cade, who was going down on one knee beside his victim. He looked up, giving her a quick assessing glance.

"Where the hell did you get the gun?" Cade asked roughly.

"It's Miss Isabel's..." Jamie broke off and started the explanation again. "I mean, Miss Isabel pulled it on me, and I knocked over the jar."

"That was the crashing sound? The cloisonné jar going over?" Cade examined Hadley's wound while the other man glared at him in helpless pain and fury.

"I threw my purse at it."

Cade's mouth crooked laconically. "I knew that forty-pound bag must be good for something. When he heard the crash and Isabel's scream, Fitzgerald lost his concentration for a moment, didn't you, Hadley? Luckily that knife I used this morning was still on the counter. I'm usually neater than that. But I guess I was feeling distracted this morning. Lie still, Fitzgerald. I'm going to take it out. Jamie, have you got a first-aid kit?"

"In the bathroom. I'll get it." Transfixed by the blood on Hadley's sleeve, Jamie backed up a couple of steps and then turned to hurry down the hall to the bathroom. When she returned to the kitchen a few minutes later, she found Cade applying pressure to staunch the bleeding.

"You're sure you're all right?" he demanded anxiously.

"I'm fine," Jamie told him again and hesitated before asking, "Where did you learn to handle a knife like that?"

"I've cleaned a lot of fish," he told her dryly. "Where did you learn to disarm people who hold guns on you?"

"I probably watched too much television in my youth."

"The hell you did. Are you sure you're all right?"

"I'm fine," she said. Jamie wondered if that was technically correct. She seemed to have developed a trembling in her fingers. Shock, she assured herself. "You're okay?"

Cade's expression was wry. "Other than being thoroughly disgusted with myself for getting you into this situation, I'm fine."

"But it wasn't your fault!" she protested, surprised.

"That's highly debatable. If I'd taken a firmer hand, listened to my hunches... Never mind. How's Miss Isabel?"

"Sitting on the bed, crying," Jamie said quietly. "If you don't need me here, I'll go to her."

"Jamie, remember where she stands in all this. At the moment she can't be your friend. She's got other priorities."

"I know, Cade. I'll be careful."

Hadley interrupted then, appealing to Cade. "Santerre, I didn't lose everything when you brought Gallagher down on me." He broke off, wincing in pain. "I've got a nice cushion stashed away in an island bank. You can have half if you'll help me get back out of the country. It's a fair-size amount. Say a hundred thousand?"

"Forget it, Fitzgerald."

"Come on, Santerre. This business you're in doesn't pay as well as I'm willing to pay. What can Gallagher give you? Five or ten grand at the most for each job."

"I've got news for you, Fitzgerald," Cade said sighing. "I haven't made a cent on you. But I have received a very valuable payoff. It's been worth the trouble." He looked at Jamie as he said the last words, and the tawny eyes were dark with meaning.

Jamie smiled back tremulously. "I've just got one question, Hadley," she said to the man on the floor. "Was it you in my room the other night?"

Hadley glowered at her. "Isabel said she'd hidden the keys in the painting. I've been watching the house. I thought her room would be empty so I went in to see if I could find them. I didn't realize you'd be sleeping in there."

"And it was you who tried to force us off the road this afternoon," Cade added, finishing his bandaging work.

"I followed you into Carmel," Hadley groaned. "When I saw you go into the bank, I knew there could be only one reason. You'd found out about the tapes.

One way or another I had to stop you and get rid of the recordings. I thought if you and the tapes all went into the sea I would be saved a great deal of effort. When that didn't work, I picked up Isabel at the motel down the road and told her we had to do whatever it took to get hold of the tapes. Then we came back here and waited for you and Jamie to arrive. Isabel wanted to try coaxing Jamie into cooperating." Hadley shot Jamie a disgusted glance. "Jamie was always so cooperative."

"Jamie and I are together now," Cade informed the older man. "That means our first loyalty is to each other."

Jamie thought about his words as she walked back down the hall to tend to Miss Isabel. *Our first loyalty is to each other*. There was no doubt in her mind about her own feelings. She had known since the affair in Santa Barbara that she was in love with Cade Santerre. She would drive herself crazy wondering if he'd declared his feelings merely to secure her cooperation. Whatever he'd done, it had been to protect her. Regardless of whether or not he really was in love, she didn't have to doubt his commitment. She sensed the strength of it and took comfort from the knowledge. It was a strong foundation on which to build, she assured herself.

It was hours before Jamie and Cade were free of the demands of the authorities who came to collect Hadley. Miss Isabel had remained behind in the big house, although she had been questioned closely. Jamie had simply refused to mention the way her former em-

ployer had held a gun on her, and Cade had allowed
her silence on the subject to stand.

"She's suffered enough," Jamie said as Cade bun-
dled her into the Mazda, which had been pulled out of
the ditch and declared operational.

"I agree." He turned the key in the ignition. "In any
event, Hadley was the dangerous one. I'm willing to
let Gallagher handle it from here on in, and as far as I
know, he only wants Fitzgerald. Got everything?"

"Yes." She looked back at the forlorn figure of Miss
Isabel standing in the doorway. "Except a job and a
good friend."

It was nearly eight o'clock that evening before Cade
finally pulled into the parking lot of a motel that promised a lounge and a restaurant. Jamie had the feeling
he'd wanted to put as many miles as possible between
them and Miss Isabel's house. She had the oddest feeling he disliked the place intensely. She didn't com-
plain. She had no desire to stay in the vicinity, either.

"God, I could use a drink." Cade climbed out of the
Mazda and stretched like a big cat. The words were almost the first he had spoken during the long drive.
"What a day. Let's get the suitcases into the room,
honey, and then head for the bar. We both deserve
something after what we've been through."

Jamie agreed wholeheartedly. She felt utterly
drained. She was tired, and she was also feeling
strangely wary. The physical exhaustion was certainly
understandable. The wariness had an explanation,
too, but she was reluctant to face it. The truth was that

during the long hours of driving, Cade had said nothing concerning his feelings for her or his plans for the future. He seemed totally preoccupied.

Well, you haven't been exactly chatty on the subject, either, she reminded herself as they found a private booth in the motel lounge. A rather bored pianist played cocktail music on the other side of the room for the small crowd.

Jamie sipped at her glass of wine and wondered why it had been easier to declare her love while facing a gun than it was now when she was alone with Cade.

Cade took two or three grateful swallows of his Scotch, his expression severe and thoughtful. When it became apparent he was not going to break the long silence, Jamie spoke.

"I won't hold you to it, you know," she murmured.

As if she'd interrupted his chain of thought, Cade frowned in mild surprise. "Hold me to what?"

"Your declaration of love this afternoon. I know you were desperate to maintain control of a very dangerous situation, and telling me you loved me was one way of doing that." She focused on the piano player across the room. She was unprepared for Cade's swift movement. He reached across the table, caught her chin and turned her to face him.

"You may not hold me to my claim of love, lady, but you can damn well bet I'm holding you to yours!"

"Cade!"

"What makes you think I didn't mean everything I said about loving you?" he demanded. "You think I go around telling women I love them just to make them cooperative? I thought you'd finally decided you could trust me."

"Yes, but..."

"So trust me!"

Jamie stared at him, unable to repress the hope that had never been very far from the surface. She had lived on that hope since this summer. "I do trust you, Cade. It's not that, it's just that I didn't want you to feel, well, obligated."

"I feel obligated," he growled. "I feel committed, obligated, and very, very determined. I've felt that way since I first met you. And since Miss Isabel slipped this afternoon and admitted it was your idea to contact me again, I've been assuming that nothing has changed for you since that time in Santa Barbara."

"Then why have you been so quiet for the past few hours?" she asked cautiously.

"I've been thinking."

"About what, for heaven's sake!"

"About what a fool I was for letting you get involved in that mess, if you want to know the truth! I've been calling myself every name in the book," he exploded softly. "Adding up all my mistakes."

"But, Cade...!"

"But nothing. I should never have played that waiting game after Santa Barbara. That was my biggest mistake. I should have refused to let you accompany Miss Isabel back to Big Sur. If I'd taken you with me when I left Santa Barbara, none of this would have happened. You would have been safe. I seem to always miscalculate around you, Jamie," he finished on a groan.

"That's probably what gave me hope for our relationship," she confided gently.

"You do want me, don't you, Jamie? I've been bouncing back and forth between heaven and hell, thinking one moment that I knew you still cared and the next that you didn't trust me. Don't put me back on that seesaw. I'll go out of my mind."

He closed his eyes in silent supplication. When he opened them again, Jamie could see the golden heat burning in the tawny gaze. "The only thing I've been absolutely certain of is how much I want you, how much I love you."

"Did you know you loved me when you walked out the door in Santa Barbara?"

"No," he admitted, his eyes never wavering in intensity. "I only knew I had to have you. I was convinced you wouldn't be able to ignore what we'd found together. I think I realized that what I was feeling was love when I found those birth-control pills in your bathroom."

Jamie blinked. "The pills?"

"That's right. When I realized just how much I'd been counting on the fact that you were pregnant, I had to really analyze my feelings. The last thing I'd ever wanted to do was get a woman with whom I was having an affair pregnant! I'd been so busy calculating, analyzing and assessing your feelings that I'd forgotten to look closely at my own. When I did, I saw the obvious truth. I love you, Jamie. I wanted you to trust me completely. It enraged me to think that you couldn't give me your complete trust. I want to make a home with you, a real home. Don't worry, I won't make you live on a fishing boat. We'll buy a nice place near the water, close enough to San Diego so that you can find another job if you like. Whatever you want. I'll do your taxes for you..."

"Joint return?" she asked softly.

He grinned briefly, a slash of sheer masculine amusement. "Most definitely a joint return. In case you haven't noticed, I'm proposing to you, Jamie Garland. All that's required from you is your acceptance."

"I will certainly give your proposal my closest consideration..."

"Jamie, don't tease me," he pleaded, the grin fading instantly. "I can't stand any more uncertainty where you're concerned."

"Having given it due consideration," she went on as if he hadn't interrupted, "I've decided to accept."

"Thank God. Jamie, you really do love me, don't you?"

"Oh, yes, Cade. I really do love you."

"I've miscalculated so frequently with you that I need the reassurance," he explained.

"Want some advice?"

"What's that?"

"Give up trying to calculate, analyze and manage me. Save your skills to use on others. Just love me, Cade. That's all that's necessary to keep me close."

"You may have a good idea there. Something seems to go awry with my skills when it comes to dealing with you, anyway." Cade reached for his wallet and tossed some bills down on the table. He got to his feet.

"Where are we going?"

"I said something happens to my business skills when I'm dealing with you," he murmured as he led her from the bar, "but my more basic instincts seem to be functioning. Come with me, my love, and let me show you just how sound my instincts are."

She went with him unprotestingly as he led her out of the lounge and up the stairs to the room. Cade's hand was warm and compelling on hers, the intensity of his grip signaling the intensity of his emotions. She sensed the fine trembling in his strong fingers as he opened the door and led her inside. Then he turned to her without bothering to switch on the light.

"Jamie, I love you so," he whispered huskily. "Please believe me."

"I do, Cade. And I trust you. I always will." Even as she said the simple words, Jamie was aware of the truth behind them. There would be no more doubts about this man. His first loyalty would always be to her, just as hers was to him. She put her arms around his neck as he began to undress her there in the darkness.

Slowly, with infinite care and tenderness, he slipped off her clothing and then his own. When they were both naked, Cade bent to lift Jamie into his arms and carry her to the bed.

Moonlight seeped through a crack in the curtains, dancing across Jamie's breasts as Cade came down beside her. He followed the path of the pale light with his fingertips, finding the tautening buds of her nipples as his mouth closed over hers.

Jamie twisted luxuriously, turning to him with gentle invitation. Her hands stroked the sleek curves of his shoulders and the bold planes of his thighs.

"Cade," she whispered throatily as he trailed his palm down her hip to the inside of her leg. "I love you so very much."

"Just go on reassuring me for the rest of my life, sweetheart. I need you. I'll always need you."

Together in the shadowy depths of the bed they explored the physical side of their love, glorying in the knowledge that there was nothing to hide, no longer any need for wariness. Jamie gave herself up to the increasingly exciting caresses. Cade's hands moved on her with unconcealed joy, parting her legs to tantalize the soft silk of her inner thighs and then moving upward to tease the sensitive flower of her passion.

"You respond so beautifully," he breathed raggedly. "You make me want to devour you." He bent his head to take a small nip at the skin of her shoulder. The wickedly exciting caress thrilled her senses. The flower he probed suddenly grew hot and moist.

His own response to her was aggressively evident. Cade's body had hardened instantly to Jamie's touch. She sensed his throbbing desire and knew he was only waiting until her own need matched his. When she moaned and instinctively closed her legs around his hand, pleading for more, he levered himself over her.

"Open for me, sweetheart. Take me inside. I need your warmth."

Willingly she put her arms around him, and then she wrapped her legs around him. Cade came down to her with an exclamation of male need, thrusting deeply into the waiting feminine heat.

"Jamie...*Jamie!*"

He held her fiercely, sharing the passionate journey totally. Jamie lost herself in Cade's embrace, knowing that he was equally lost in her arms. They clung together, abandoning themselves to the ancient rhythm, until the tightening sensation within them burst into a thrilling, convulsive release. And then they rode the descending path as one, united physically and emotionally.

Afterward Jamie lay enmeshed in the soft intimacy. She was vaguely aware of Cade's leg thrown across her thighs and of his quiet breath fanning her ear as he lay beside her. She knew he was awake and that he was lazily studying her face in the shadows. With a faint smile she turned to him.

"What are you thinking?" she whispered, stroking his arm with her fingertips.

"I was wondering why I made so many mistakes during this crazy courtship," he answered wryly.

She grinned. "Ah, that's because deep down there's a very strong romantic streak in you."

He glowered at her with mock ferocity. "Nonsense. I've been a rational, pragmatic man all my life. You're the romantic, not me."

"Rational, pragmatic businessmen do not throw away successful careers in order to go live on a boat," Jamie pointed out calmly.

"I've explained that," he began on a note of protest.

"Oh, you've worked up some reasons, but nothing can disguise the basically romantic impulse. You fell victim to the call of the sea and the lure of adventure. You want another example? How about the way you took two whole months to get me into bed this summer?"

"What about it?" he asked suspiciously.

"Wonderfully romantic," she breathed in fond memory.

"I just wanted everything to be right, that's all."

"It was. It was perfect. Only a true romantic would devote that much attention to the details of a seduction," Jamie teased.

"Afterward you thought I'd just been spinning a web."

"Well, you were in a way. A romantic web. And then there was the way you assumed after only one night with me that I was probably pregnant. Only a true romantic would so completely convince himself of that without proof. You actually wanted me to be pregnant. Very endearing. And then there was the way you chased after me when I left your marina the other morning. Fantastically romantic. Then, of course, you topped it all off by saving my neck."

"I think you may be interpreting events in the light of your own distinctly rosy view of life," Cade complained good-naturedly.

"Not at all. Cade, you've done an excellent job of hiding your basic romantic impulses beneath a veneer of hard-headed pragmatism, but underneath you're a lot like me. It's only natural that when you ran into another romantic you'd have trouble predicting and manipulating her actions."

"I fail to follow the logic of that."

"Romance and love have no logic," she informed him wisely.

"You've got an answer for everything, don't you?" he asked admiringly.

She laughed softly. "I'm working on it."

"There's one small detail you're forgetting."

"What's that?"

"I was right about one thing: you did come looking for me after that scene in Santa Barbara. Miss Isabel said it was all your idea, remember?"

"Are you going to hold that over my head for the rest of my life?" she complained.

"Probably. But I won't tease you about it right now. I've got better things to do."

"Such as?" she challenged throatily, her fingers stroking languidly down his chest.

"I'm going to put a few of my romantic impulses into practice." Cade lowered his head and kissed the hollow of her throat.

Jamie felt the renewed tautness in his body, sensed the rising hunger in him. "This is romance?"

"The hell with romance. This is love."

She didn't doubt him. Cade Santerre might not recognize the genuine streak of romance in his soul, but he knew all about the important things in life.

The spellbinding story of a man and woman who journey through hell to arrive at a place in their hearts that offers the promise of heaven.

THE DEVIL'S OWN

In a terrifying race to save nine children from the threat of war-torn Central America, Kerry Bishop prepared for the fight of her life. But she wasn't prepared for a passion almost as dangerous as the mission she had undertaken.

Dependent on a stranger, Kerry refused to let unexpected desire complicate their mission. Survival was all they could think about. But if they succeeded, what then?

NEW YORK TIMES BESTSELLING AUTHOR

SANDRA BROWN

Available March 2001
wherever hardcovers are sold!

MIRA®

MSB793

New York Times **Bestselling Author**

JOAN JOHNSTON

Abigail Dayton has a job to do—trap and relocate a wolf that is threatening local ranches, in an effort to save the species from extinction. Abby knows the breed well: powerful, strong and lean. As rare as it is beautiful. Aggressive when challenged. A predator.

But the description fits both the endangered species she's sworn to protect...and a man she's determined to avoid. Local rancher Luke Granger is a lone wolf, the kind of man who doesn't tame or trust easily. The kind of man who tempts a woman to risk everything....

Never Tease a Wolf

Available April 2001 wherever paperbacks are sold!

**Secrets, lies, blame and guilt.
Only love and forgiveness can overcome
the mistakes of the past.**

RACHEL LEE

Witt Matlock has carried around a bitter hatred for Hardy
Wingate, the man he holds responsible for the death of his
daughter. And now, twelve years later, the man he blames for
the tragedy is back in his life—and in that of his niece, Joni.

Widow Hannah Matlock has kept the truth about her
daughter Joni's birth hidden for twenty-seven years. Only she
knows that her brother-in-law Witt is Joni's father, and not
her uncle. But with Hardy coming between Witt and Joni,
Hannah knows she must let go of her secret...whatever the
consequences.

A JANUARY CHILL

"A magnificent presence in romantic fiction.
Rachel Lee is an author to treasure forever."
—*Romantic Times*

On sale April 2001 wherever paperbacks are sold!

MRL802

JAYNE ANN KRENTZ

66624	MAN WITH A PAST	___ $6.99 U.S.	___ $8.50 CAN.
66595	BETWEEN THE LINES	___ $6.99 U.S.	___ $8.50 CAN.
66640	TEST OF TIME	___ $6.99 U.S.	___ $8.50 CAN.
66639	JOY	___ $6.99 U.S.	___ $8.50 CAN.
66563	CALL IT DESTINY	___ $5.99 U.S.	___ $6.99 CAN.
66555	THE FAMILY WAY	___ $5.99 U.S.	___ $6.99 CAN.
66524	GHOST OF A CHANCE	___ $5.99 U.S.	___ $6.99 CAN.
66494	THE COWBOY	___ $5.99 U.S.	___ $6.99 CAN.
66462	THE ADVENTURER	___ $6.99 U.S.	___ $7.99 CAN.
66437	THE PIRATE	___ $6.99 U.S.	___ $7.99 CAN.
66315	A WOMAN'S TOUCH	___ $6.99 U.S.	___ $7.99 CAN.
66270	LADY'S CHOICE	___ $6.99 U.S.	___ $7.99 CAN.
66158	WITCHCRAFT	___ $5.99 U.S.	___ $6.99 CAN.
66148	LEGACY	___ $5.99 U.S.	___ $6.99 CAN.

(limited quantities available)

TOTAL AMOUNT	$_____
POSTAGE & HANDLING	$_____
($1.00 for one book; 50¢ for each additional)	
APPLICABLE TAXES*	$_____
<u>TOTAL PAYABLE</u>	$_____
(check or money order—please do not send cash)	

To order, complete this form and send it, along with a check or money order for the total above, payable to MIRA Books®, to: **In the U.S.:** 3010 Walden Avenue, P.O. Box 9077, Buffalo, NY 14269-9077; **In Canada:** P.O. Box 636, Fort Erie, Ontario L2A 5X3.

Name:_____

Address:_____ City:_____

State/Prov.:_____ Zip/Postal Code:_____

Account Number (if applicable):_____

075 CSAS

*New York residents remit applicable sales taxes.
Canadian residents remit applicable
GST and provincial taxes.

Visit us at www.mirabooks.com   MJAK0301BL